Tales of the Were
Grizzly Cove
Crossroads

Bounty Hunter Bear

BIANCA D'ARC

DEDICATION

To the amazing doctors and staff at St. Francis Hospital who have saved my Dad's life time and again. I can't thank you all enough. As I write this dedication, Dad is recovering from surgery and will be home shortly, thanks to the skilled aid of everyone at the hospital and, as Dad would say, "the good Lord."

So this book is dedicated to Dad and to those who saved his life, again. Even though they'll probably never see it and Dad certainly won't be reading any of my romance titles! But, even so, I wanted to make special mention because it means a lot to me.

I also want to thank my friends and fans who have been so incredibly supportive. You guys are the best! Special thanks to Penny Scarangella and Peggy McChesney. Super thanks to my long-time editor, Jess Bimberg. Any remaining mistakes, typos, and/or blunders, are completely my fault. LOL!

CHAPTER ONE

Nothing could compare to the feel of the open road. His beloved Harley beneath him, the asphalt spinning away under its tires as the miles ticked by. Freedom. That's what it was. Pure, undiluted, unobstructed freedom.

Traveling when he felt like it, instead of on orders. Going where the wind took him, sleeping under the stars, or in the rain. Hell, he wasn't picky, and as a grizzly bear shifter, he could sleep just about anywhere, and under almost any conditions, in his fur.

The only limitation was that he had to check in if he planned to stay any length of time in a territory ruled by another Clan, Pack or Tribe. Most were understanding when he explained his business and that he had zero interest in challenging anyone for their territory. Occasionally, he crossed paths with a complete asshole, and then, he had to show them—physically—who was the bigger badass. He did his best to avoid conflict, but if it came to him, he was more than able to deal with it.

Ezra Tate hadn't been one of Uncle Sam's best and brightest killers for most of his life to put up with petty crap from lesser bears who just wanted to flex their muscles. He didn't play power games. Not anymore. His tolerance for bullshit had all but disappeared after the career-ending—nearly life-ending—injury he'd suffered in some foreign hellhole with more sand than common sense.

These days he was his own bear. He'd coasted from place to place, working as a bounty hunter, for the past few years, but just lately, he'd taken up work with a bear he respected named Trevor, and his new mate, a pretty little mermaid named Beth. Ezra had been chasing a bounty up along the coastline of Washington State when he'd run smack into the middle of a situation in which he had to choose sides.

He'd chosen to protect the mermaid with the huge price on her head because she was Trevor's mate. Trev had always been a straight shooter, and they'd been both comrades and friends in Uncle Sam's Special Forces. Trev had gone to work for Major Moore, who was running a shifter merc group off his mountaintop in Wyoming, but Ezra had needed space to roam.

Moore was a werewolf, and he needed Pack around him, while Ezra's bear had craved freedom. He'd figured eventually, after bounty hunting had lost its allure or he ran out of cash—whichever happened first—he'd probably go ask Moore for a job, but he'd never expected to turn in his bounty hunting career to go corporate.

But that's just what he'd done when it turned out Trevor's new mate was an heiress in dire need of help cleaning up the mess her stepfather had left behind. Beth's stepdaddy had been a real shark. Literally. A shark shifter named Jonathan, who had kept Beth's mother a veritable prisoner on Catalina Island. It had been Jonathan who'd put a really high price on Beth's head when she was about to come of age and inherit her real father's holdings.

Holdings that Jonathan had been using for illegal purposes for years. You name the sleazy business, and that shark asshole had been into it. Prostitution, drugs, even human trafficking. In fact, Ezra had helped a werewolf woman who worked for the famous shifter private eye, Collin Hastings, just a few months back.

Margo, the werewolf investigator and her mate, a powerful mage named Gabe, had roared into Lake Tahoe hot on the trail of a real son of a bitch mage who'd caused a whole lot of problems for Margo's Pack up in Canada. Ezra had been able to help them stop the mage, while at the same time freeing a number of women who'd been kidnapped from all across the United States by some of Jonathan's former colleagues.

Ezra had taken great satisfaction in helping shut down that particular operation. He'd cleansed the area—and the businesses owned by Beth and Trevor—of Jonathan's evil taint. He'd also helped take down the mage who had kept five of the women prisoner in a nondescript gray house that had been a hellhole of torture and despair.

The five women were magical in some way. Most had been human with some small gifts of magic that the mage had hoped to siphon away along with their lives. The other woman...

The other woman had been a bear shifter. Theodora. That was her name.

Ezra could still remember the feel of her emaciated body in his arms as he pulled her from the basement prison where she and the other women had been held. She'd been in rough shape. Her bear had been all but dead, drained to the point of possibly no return by the bastard mage called Bolivar. Ezra had witnessed the man being blown to atoms in front of his eyes, but every time he thought about how bad off Theodora was, he wished he could kill the bastard again. Painfully.

Ezra had been unable to let go of her. Even as they rode in a van to a safe house—or rather, a safe *mansion*—that was also owned by his employers, he'd found it nearly impossible to let her go. When they'd arrived at the house, he'd carried her to the waiting medical people and stayed with her as long as he possibly could. He'd watched over her sleep. He'd even been there when she woke a few times, his inner bear calming what was left of hers.

He was a strong Alpha. He wasn't sure what sort of bear she'd once been, but if she survived with her spirit animal intact after a period of healing, he hoped she would be a force to be reckoned with. He wasn't sure, though. It could go either way.

Ezra had always been of the frame of mind that what doesn't kill you makes you stronger, but he was a guy. A soldier. The only easy day was yesterday had been his motto for a very long time. Theodora... By all accounts, she'd been a girly-girl. The apple of her parents' eyes.

He'd been able to reunite her with her folks, and he'd been moved by the family reunion that had taken place at the mansion in the hills above Lake Tahoe. Her folks had been flown out special delivery, as it were, under the auspices of the shifter P.I., Collin Hastings. Thea's folks had hired Collin to find their missing daughter, so he'd been able to contact them right away once they realized she had been held in that basement of horrors.

Ezra's inner bear had whined when Thea's parents had loaded her into a van and driven her away. He'd only known her for a few hours—a day or two at most between rescuing her, getting her to the mansion and reuniting her with her parents—but he felt more than a little proprietary where she was concerned. That wasn't usual for him.

He tried to tell himself it was just the circumstances. Her rescue had been dramatic. Her condition had been criminal. That she was a fellow bear shifter spoke to his inner animal on a very basic level. That she was a lovely woman—badly emaciated but still showing signs of an ethereal beauty that had haunted his dreams ever since—was just icing on the cake.

Ezra liked pretty women. What red-blooded man didn't? But it was more than just her looks. Thea's vulnerability made him mad. What had been done to her—the systematic siphoning of her natural magical power—enraged him on a whole new level of anger. He knew it wasn't a good thing to operate from such an emotional place, but he couldn't help it.

He tried really hard to be objective. To be the disinterested soldier sent to do a job. But it didn't work. Not with Thea. There was just something about her...

Of course, chances were, their paths would never cross again. Ezra was very tempted to look her up, but he hesitated. He didn't want to drag up memories of an episode in her life that she was probably still trying to put behind her. It had been a few months now, but he knew that recovery from the kind of magical injuries she had sustained could take *years*.

And Ezra was kept very busy cleaning up the huge mess of corruption and criminal behavior left behind by Beth's unlamented stepfather, Jonathan. Ezra was based out of Grizzly Cove, up on the Washington coast, these days, but his work took him all over. He and his faithful Harley had been up and down the West Coast, settling affairs and putting Beth and Trevor's businesses back to rights. Putting them back to more *legal* endeavors with honest people at the helms of the various companies.

He'd done a lot of house cleaning, business by business. He'd turned more than one miscreant over to the human authorities for nice fat bounties. He'd kept his cover as a bounty hunter. Only Beth, Trevor, Ezra and a few of the leaders back in Grizzly Cove knew that Ezra was really working for the couple. Beth and Trev didn't mind if Ezra collected the bounties, as long as Beth's father's legacy was put to rights in the process, so it was a win-win, as Beth would say.

If anyone had said Ezra was going to be friends with a mermaid, he would've told them to have their heads examined, but sure enough, he counted Beth and Trev among his closest friends now. He'd always been close to Trevor, of course, but Ezra hadn't really been sure about Beth at first. He'd been willing to give her the benefit of the doubt because she was Trev's mate, but his tolerance had soon turned to admiration. Beth was a perfect match for Ezra's old buddy, and he was happy for them.

He just didn't know if he'd ever find a mate of his own.

He'd had a good long, hard look around Grizzly Cove. There were a lot of pretty mermaids living in the cove now that the Alpha bear had offered sanctuary to a mer pod that had been under attack out at sea. Somehow, the bear shifters who had founded the small town were getting along like gangbusters with the usually reclusive mer folk.

While Ezra had seen more than one pretty mermaid he might want to date, none roused his inner bear. None of them had been his mate.

No one had brought his bear to hyper awareness except Theodora. But whether it was a sign that she could be his mate or merely his bear's outrage at what had been done to her, he wasn't quite sure. He'd definitely felt something for her, but whether it was the draw of a mate, he didn't know. Maybe someday... When she was healed from her ordeal... Maybe he'd look her up and see if there was anything that might blossom between them.

Then again, maybe he'd just leave the poor girl alone and not show up as a big, fat reminder of what had to be one of the worst experiences of her life. Yeah, that would probably be kinder.

*

Thea loved the feeling of the wind on her body, against the leather clothing that she wore for protection...and because she liked the way it looked. The way it made her feel. Like nothing could touch her. Nothing could harm her.

She thought she probably looked like a total badass in her leathers, on her new bike. Just like the woman who'd helped free her and so many other women who had been caught up in a human trafficking trap.

Margo. That was the name of the woman who'd made such a big impression on Thea in those few days she'd stayed in the mansion above Lake Tahoe, healing. Margo might be a werewolf, but she was a force to be reckoned with, in her own right. Thea had talked with Margo a few times before she left in the care of her parents, and she'd grown to respect the woman who had found her mate in a very powerful mage who had gone toe to toe with the bastard that had almost killed Thea.

She would be forever in the couple's debt. They'd put themselves at risk to help her and all those other women who'd been held prisoner. They, along with their team of colleagues, had executed a coordinated strike, Thea had come to learn, on three different hotels that were holding human women captured by the slavery ring and the house of horrors in which Thea and four other women had been held.

All the women in that basement prison had been magical, though Thea had been the only shifter. Maybe that's why the mage had tortured her first. She wasn't sure, and she'd probably never know why Bolivar had taken such delight in torturing her inner bear almost to death.

But she was free now. Free and on the mend. Her parents had worried about Thea taking off on her own, but she couldn't take any more of their coddling. She'd changed on a fundamental level in that hellish basement. She'd been nearly destroyed and had reformed over the past few months. She'd come back stronger, and she wanted to be stronger still. Part of that ongoing recovery process was learning all over again how to trust herself, and this solo journey across several states was a big step forward on that trail.

There had been another who had been part of her rescue and had left a lasting impression. A big man. A bear shifter named Ezra.

He'd been her anchor in those dark hours just after she'd been freed. He'd held her from the moment he'd lifted her out of the cage she'd been kept in for so long she'd lost count of the days, until she passed out. And he'd been there every time she'd awoken. His strong Alpha presence had soothed her inner bear, which had been drained so badly it had almost left her completely. But Ezra had given her inner bear hope to go on, to recover, to get stronger, and more powerful than it had been before her ordeal.

She had so much to thank him for. Only... She wasn't sure he'd even remember her. Or, if he did, she worried that he'd think of her as that pitiful creature he'd rescued from hell.

She didn't want to see pity in his eyes if they ever met again. She knew she should just forget him. The likelihood that they would cross paths was low. Chances were, she'd never see him again. And yet... She couldn't really stop thinking about him.

She wasn't sure why that was. He was a compelling being, and he'd done her a very great favor in rescuing her. He'd grounded her—and especially her inner bear—at the most critical moment in her life so far. She would be forever grateful to him for that, and for the fierce way he'd overseen her medical treatment while she'd been at that mansion.

Oh, he hadn't been all that obvious about it, but she'd known he was always there in the background whenever she was left with the medical personnel and healers. He'd be just outside in the hallway, waiting for the all-clear to come back in. He'd probably been neglecting everyone else, just to make sure her bear was all right. He must have sensed how much on the brink she'd been of losing her bear half forever.

She credited Ezra with saving that side of her being. If not for his strong Alpha presence to cling to, her inner bear might just have given up the fight right then and there. She wasn't sure what that would have meant for her human half. Death, probably. She wasn't sure a shifter could exist without her beast or vice versa.

So, Ezra had really saved her life twice over. First, by rescuing her from that prison and then by not allowing her to slip into oblivion. His bear had coaxed hers to stay. To heal and to give the medical people a chance to help her. Ezra was the reason she was still alive. And she didn't even know his last name.

CHAPTER TWO

Ezra was heading for South Dakota, to meet up with some specialist help he'd convinced to come from Phoenix. The three mechanics were brothers, and all were grizzly shifters. Ezra had met them years ago, and when he followed the far-reaching threads of Beth's business interests all the way to South Dakota and the famous motorcycle rally held there each year, he knew just who to ask for assistance.

The brothers owed him. He'd saved their asses more than once on overseas ops. They'd all served together, and all being bears, they'd sort of gravitated together in the Special Forces unit that had been made up of all sorts of shifters. They'd drifted apart over the years since getting out of the military, but those bonds were never broken. The men kept in touch from time to time, and they all knew that, if one of them needed help, they could always call on the others.

As Ezra had done in this particular instance. The brothers were experienced mechanics with serious resumes. They could get into places that Ezra didn't have the credentials to penetrate himself. They could get behind the scenes more easily and scope out the extent of the problem in the business

Ezra was trying to investigate on his employer's behalf.

Trevor knew the brothers and had approved their temporary addition to the troubleshooting team Ezra ran. Most of the time, the squad was just him, but on occasion, when he needed specialist assistance, he was authorized to spend a bit for expertise.

The brothers had flown from their current base in Phoenix to South Dakota and were already nosing around. The plan was for Ezra to meet them there later in the week to find out what they'd learned so far and make plans for their next steps. To add some authenticity to his arrival, Ezra was riding across a few states, starting out in Grizzly Cove and ending in the motorcycle heaven that was South Dakota during rally week.

He might be going there to do a job, but that didn't mean he couldn't enjoy the trip. He'd taken Interstate 90 across and was in Wyoming. The land was rugged and breathtaking, and Ezra was glad he'd chosen to do the long trip. It had been too long since it was just him and his bike and the open road. He liked the steady gig with Beth and Trevor, but he was also a bear who liked his freedom. Trevor understood that, being a bear himself, so he was a good boss for a guy like Ezra.

When he rode through the outskirts of a small town with a truck stop, Ezra figured it was about time to stop and refuel—both the bike and his body. A truck stop meal might not be cordon bleu, but it would keep you going. He figured he was about halfway through Wyoming at this point. He had a few more hours to go until he crossed over into South Dakota. Luckily, his target wasn't that far from the border, so if all continued to go well, he'd be checking into the hotel he'd reserved on time.

After a few days on the road, he was looking forward to a soft bed and a warm shower. Who knew? He might even try out the indoor pool and hot tub the hotel featured prominently on their website. Warm water on stiff muscles sounded really good to a guy who'd been sitting on a bike for several hundred miles.

He'd need all his wits about him when he finally got his teeth into the problem he'd come to solve. One of the businesses Beth had inherited was a small garage in South Dakota, oddly enough, that did a brisk business every year during the motorcycle rally. It did decent business the rest of the year, too, but like many of the businesses in that town, it peaked during the rally.

Ezra suspected the garage was using its rapid turnover of imported parts and engines to camouflage smuggling operations. Being so near the Canadian border also meant that drugs were probably being brought up through Mexico, stopping off in that garage then making their way across the border to the North.

If that was the case—and Ezra had already collected some pretty damning evidence on paper—then he was going to clean house. First, though, he had to verify the operation was still running drugs and find out exactly which employees were involved and how deeply. If they were shifters, he would mete out justice the old-fashioned way. If they were human, he'd have to get creative in how he handled getting them caught for something without implicating the garage as a whole. The business itself should be salvageable, and that was Ezra's goal—preserving as many of his employers' assets as possible while cleaning them all up and ending any illegal activity.

Ezra parked his bike where he could see it from the window of the truck stop and walked inside. He'd fuel up before he left, but for right now, he needed food and plenty of it. He headed toward the restaurant area and chose a seat at the window that gave him a good view of all the exits, as well as outside. When the waitress sashayed over and took his order, he gave her a smile as she filled his coffee cup. A few minutes later, after he'd sent a quick text to his friend Ace to apprise him that Ezra was right on schedule, the food came, and Ezra began to shovel it in.

It smelled decent. The food at this particular truck stop was a bit better than at the chain places. He scented fresh herbs and vegetables in his generous portion of meatloaf, and the gravy was tasty. He applied himself to his meal, and other than glancing occasionally at his bike, he let the food begin to wash away some of his weariness.

It wasn't until he was mopping up the last of his dessert that Ezra heard the rumble of an approaching motorcycle engine. It was a newer model Harley in prime condition, and as it pulled into a spot right next to his bike, he noticed the female driving it was pretty prime herself. A shapely ass and long legs made his mouth water as she stood from her ride as if she'd been born to straddle that hog.

She took off her helmet and looped it over the handle, shaking out long golden hair that made him think of honey. And, of course, bears *loved* honey. The woman was a knockout from behind in her leather duds that hugged every curve faithfully. Then she, turned and started walking toward the entrance.

It couldn't be.

No fucking way.

The last time he'd seen that beautiful face, it had been gaunt with weight loss, and her energy had been at its lowest ebb. Could the bombshell with the curves that didn't quit and the smooth sashay that said she owned her piece of the world and Goddess help anyone who tried to take it from her be the same woman he'd rescued those months ago in Lake Tahoe?

Could it really be Theodora?

His heart almost stopped as she opened the door and headed straight for the restaurant. She gazed around the room, taking it all in, and Ezra found himself standing without even thinking about it. Their gazes met across the distance and held…

Her eyes narrowed for a moment, but she didn't make any other outward show. Then, she started walking toward him.

Goddess help him. It really was Theodora, and she was heading his way.

She looked long and lean and curvy in all the right places. As she drew nearer, he caught the delicate scent of her on the air-conditioned currents. She smelled even better than she had before, if that was even possible. Sure, she'd been weak and had almost given up the ghost a couple of times before she stabilized and started to come back to the land of the living, but he'd remembered her delicate scent. A scent that had haunted him these many months.

And now, she was here. How? Why?

Ezra almost shook his head. Did it really matter? She was here, and she had recognized him. Well, that answered that question. She remembered him. More than that, she remembered him and hadn't run screaming in the other direction at the sight of him. Will wonders never cease?

Thea walked right up to him and stopped, a few feet separating them. She looked him straight in the eye, strong, vibrant. So different from the way she'd been when he'd last seen her flying away in the company of her parents on a private plane chartered by Collin Hastings.

"Ezra." Her voice was solid. Full of confidence that seemed to ooze from her every move. It was incredibly sexy.

"Theodora," he replied, nodding slightly. "You're looking well," he said, then thought his words a little too sappy. "You're looking incredible, in fact."

"Thanks to you," she replied after a moment where she shifted her weight from one foot to the other, drawing his attention to her lusciously curved hips. "I can't recall if I ever did thank you properly for what you did."

Ezra held up one hand, palm outward. "No need. I'm just glad I was there, in the right place, at the right time."

She looked like she wanted to argue the point, but her gaze flitted around the room. People were watching them. *Right. Get a grip, man.*

"Would you like to join me?" he asked, gesturing toward the other side of the booth he'd been sitting in for the better part of an hour.

"I don't want to intrude," she said, but he hoped she was just being polite.

"Not at all. I'd enjoy the company," he told her. If he'd

been at a table with actual chairs, he would've acted the gentleman and pulled one out for her, coercing her to sit with him. As it was, he merely stood, waiting for her to make up her mind.

She finally took a seat, sliding into the booth opposite him, and he let go of the breath he hadn't realized he'd been holding. He sat back down and signaled the waitress to bring more coffee and a menu for the lady. If the waitress seemed disappointed that Ezra had found female companionship, he tried not to notice.

Thea couldn't believe she was sitting opposite the man who had saved her life all those months ago and who had featured pretty heavily in her dreams ever since.

Ezra. That's all she knew him as. She didn't know his last name. She didn't know where he'd come from or where he'd gone to after she left Lake Tahoe. Many times, she'd been tempted to try to figure out a way to look him up, but so far, she'd been able to curb her impulses.

No need for that anymore. He was right here. Sitting with her. She could hardly believe it.

He was as tall and handsome as she remembered. His face was angular, and his eyes were a golden brown that seemed to go on forever. His shoulders were even broader than she remembered, which was saying something, and he filled out his denim jeans really, *really* well, from what she'd been able to observe.

In short, he was hot with a capital H.O.T.

She thought maybe she'd been dreaming how handsome he was. How Alpha. In her weakened state, she could have easily attributed traits to her rescuer that weren't true, but she was astounded to realize that she hadn't done that at all. No, Ezra of the no-last-name was everything she remembered…and more.

His presence didn't intimidate her. He never had, which was a marvel, considering how she'd been before her ordeal. While not exactly submissive on the level of some other

14

species of shifter, for a bear, Thea had been rather weak-kneed before her abduction and torture.

Now? Well, she wasn't quite sure where that experience had left her. That was part of the reason she was on the road, going walkabout, seeking answers to what she was now, after the months she'd spent healing.

Whatever it was, she was no longer the timid, submissive bear she'd once been. Was she more Alpha? Well, she wasn't quite sure about that. She didn't feel like kicking everyone's ass all the time—which was what she supposed Alphas must feel like, based on the limited exposure she'd had to the local Alpha bear in her parent's area. He wasn't in their territory, per se, but a loner who lived on the edge of their land. They didn't have much to do with each other, each preferring to roam alone, or in the case of her folks, just with each other and their only cub.

She felt bad about leaving them, but they'd understood her reasons, even if they would rather have had her stay. She would go back, but not right away. She had a bit of self-discovery to do, and she didn't think she could do it in the safe embrace of her familial home. If she'd stayed there, she would've reverted to a younger mindset. She probably would've let her parents take care of her, as they had when she was truly a child.

The healthiest thing for her development right now was to have a little solo adventure. The priestess she'd been talking to since her rescue had heartily approved of her idea to go it alone for a month or two and had helped break the news to her parents. They'd taken it better than Thea had expected and had seen her off with tears—on her mother's part—but also with their best wishes for her growth, healing and safe return.

Thea had never imagined when she set out a week ago that she'd be sitting in a truck stop diner, facing the devastatingly handsome bear shifter who had rescued her. Not in a million years could she have imagined this scenario, but she was going to take advantage of it. She wanted to know more about him, and this might be her only chance to talk to him.

"So, where are you headed?" she asked after the waitress had come and delivered more coffee for him and taken Thea's order.

She realized pretty quickly that Ezra must have already eaten, but he'd ordered something, probably just to keep her company. She liked that. He wasn't going to let her eat alone and feel self-conscious about it, nice guy that he was.

"I'm going up to Sturgis for the rally," he answered easily, but she sensed there was more to his simple words than met the eye.

Still, she wouldn't pry here. Not in the middle of a busy diner with all these people around. People who were mostly—if her senses didn't deceive her—humans with no clue about the shifters peppered among them.

"I was heading that way myself," she admitted. "I got a new bike, and the guys at the shop couldn't stop talking about the rally, so I decided to come see what it was all about."

"Just like that?" Ezra asked, his golden-brown gaze speaking of his interest.

"Yeah, just like that," she affirmed. "Ever since... Well... You know. Ever since then, I've been craving freedom, and this trip is a bit of a vision quest type thing, except without the peyote," she joked. He chuckled along with her as the waitress deposited her food in front of her.

"I'm glad for you. You look like you've recovered really well," he said gently, his eyes crinkling up at the corners in a kind smile. He might be a fierce Alpha bear, but he'd always been kind to her.

"I'm better. Physically, I've recovered," she told him honestly. If anyone deserved to know what was going on with her since her rescue, it was him. "Mentally... Well... Things have changed a lot for me. Part of taking this trip is to figure out what I am now, if that makes any sense."

Ezra nodded. "It makes perfect sense. You know..." He leaned forward, their conversation kept to low tones that wouldn't carry beyond their table. "I spent a lot of years in the military. Certain experiences can impact a person in ways you don't fully understand until you've had time to figure it all out. Talking with my buddies about some of the things we went through together helped. Spending time on my own helped, too. You're doing that now, and I think that's healthy, but if you ever need to talk, I'm here for you. Or maybe you could talk to some of the other women," he suggested without going into detail. She knew who he meant. The other women who'd been held prisoner by Bolivar in his basement of horrors.

She nodded, swallowing hard. "I'm still in contact with them, and I've been talking to our local wise woman ever since I got back home. My parents have been great. They're very supportive, even if they don't fully understand why I packed my saddlebags and took off on this journey." She smiled as she thought of her folks. "But I do appreciate the offer. However, I don't even know your last name. It's kind of hard to call someone when you don't know their name or number."

She chuckled, wondering if he'd be cagey about his personal data. Some shifter men were squirrely when it came to giving out the digits, preferring to be phantoms.

Ezra grinned. "Sorry, Thea. I'm Ezra Tate. I didn't really think about the fact that we never got around to a formal introduction."

He extended his hand across the table, and she took it for a friendly shake. She tried hard to ignore the sexy little sizzle of sensation going up her arm from where their hands met. The man should come with a warning label. Really.

When their hands parted—after just a hint too long for a casual handshake—she missed his touch. That was unexpected. Hmm.

"You probably already know all about me, right?" Thea asked, feeling a tad self-conscious.

"Yeah, I admit, your folks provided a profile to Collin, the private eye they hired to find you," he told her. "I read the file when we were searching for you and the others," he admitted. "You were a teacher, right?"

"Primary school. I worked with little kids, and I loved it. But, when I disappeared, my job disappeared, too, and I haven't had the heart to look for another. I'm not sure I'm ready to go back to work yet," she said, surprising herself with her honesty. It had taken some time for her to admit that truth to herself, and even longer to tell her parents.

"Nothing wrong with taking a little time to reassess," he said.

She tried to read his expression, to see if he was as disappointed with her decision as her mother had seemed. She didn't see anything on his face to indicate that his words weren't meant to be taken at face value, which made her feel a little better. Her mom had seemed so worried when Thea had finally admitted that she didn't want to go back to work in the fall.

She applied herself to her meal for a few minutes. The silence was companionable. Ezra was an easy person to be around. He made her feel safe.

And sort of tingly… In a good way.

"So, are you meeting friends in town?" Ezra asked her after a while.

"No. I don't know anybody there. I just figured I'd check out the rally and see what it was all about. The cougars at my bike shop couldn't stop talking about how awesome it was."

"Did you line up a place to stay?" he asked, frowning a bit.

"Well, I figured I'd just find a place when I got there," she admitted, sensing maybe she hadn't thought her plan all the way through when his frown deepened.

"The town really fills up during the event," he told her. "There might not be any rooms left."

"Seriously?" She hadn't anticipated that. She knew next to nothing about the town or the rally. It had just sounded like as good a destination as any when she'd set out on her motorcycle vision quest minus the peyote.

"Look, uh…" He seemed a little uncomfortable, but he went on as she waited. "I'm going there on business. I've reserved a suite, which I might not even be using most of the time. If you can't find a place, you're welcome to crash with me. I mean—not *with* me—but in the suite. I'm not trying to hit on you or make you uncomfortable, but I can't, in good conscience, leave you to fend for yourself when I have a big room all set aside that I may not even be using most of the time."

Now, it was her turn to frown. He'd been almost tongue-tied there for a moment. Was she that repulsive? Or that needy? She didn't like either scenario. Her newfound backbone stiffened.

"I appreciate the offer but—"

Ezra held up one hand, cutting her off. "I said that badly," he told her, shaking his head. "I want to be sure you've got a safe place, Thea. For my own peace of mind, as well as your safety. The town can get a little wild with the influx of people. I'd be pleased if you'd just take my room. I can try to find another if you'd rather not have me around."

"Not have you around? Is that what you think?" She was shocked by his words. "Ezra, you saved my life. How could I not want to have you around? At this point, you're like the one person in the world, besides my parents, that I trust fully. If you'd wanted to hurt me, you would have left me in that basement. Or you could have let me die when I was so weak. But you stayed, and you fought for me. I could feel your power reaching out to me, willing me to live," she told him in a desperate whisper that went no farther than their small booth. "The fact that you're willing to help me again, when it's pretty clear I didn't think this trip all the way through, just proves all over again that you're one of the good guys. If you're sure you don't mind, I might just take you up on your generous offer."

"Now, wait a minute." He held up both hands, palms outward. "Don't go polishing my halo so shiny." His lips curled up at the corners, softening his denial. "You'll ruin my image."

She laughed with him, and balance was restored between

them. He really was an easy guy to be around. She wasn't sure she'd ever felt so comfortable with another bear—besides her family, of course. She didn't know what it meant, but it felt significant.

"So, is that what you do?" she asked, returning to a previous point in the conversation. "You work for the private investigation firm my parents hired?"

"No, not at all. I'm actually a bounty hunter. Or, at least, I was until recently," he clarified. "See? I don't really deserve that halo. I deal with the worst of the worst, usually. I was just helping Margo—who really is a P.I." He took a sip of his coffee before continuing. "Just between us, I'm a troubleshooter now. I clean up dirty businesses."

"Is that why you're going to Sturgis?" she asked quietly.

He nodded. "Yeah. My employer owns a business there that I suspect is being used for something... Well... Something bad. I'm here to put a stop to it. I'm telling you this because, if you're going to stay in my suite, you might need to be aware of what's going on. I don't intend for anything to spill over, but it doesn't hurt to be cautious. The people I'll be dealing with can be dangerous."

"It's not like what was happening in Tahoe, is it?" she asked breathlessly.

"No, not at all," he answered quickly. "It's something else." He looked around, as if considering how much to tell her, then caught her eye again. "Let's just say that if you really wanted that peyote for the vision quest, these guys could probably get it for you."

"Drugs?" she whispered, surprised but intensely relieved the activity he was tracking wasn't related to human trafficking.

Ezra nodded. "Smuggling them over the northern border. Or so I believe," he added casually.

To any observers, their conversation probably looked totally normal—at least on Ezra's part. She took her cue from him and tried to relax her features. Not that she thought anyone was really watching them, but why take chances?

They were close enough to their destination now that there were a lot of motorcycles on the road with them. In fact, many were parked in front of the truck stop, and they probably belonged to a number of the people sitting all around them.

Thea applied herself to the last bits of her meal and finished just as the waitress returned to ask if she wanted anything else. She declined anything sweet, knowing she'd gained a bit too much weight since her rescue. Ezra seemed like he wanted to say something about her choice but didn't, and the waitress left the bill on the table. Ezra snatched it up before Thea could, and they had a little discussion about how she wanted to pay her way.

He won, of course. He just simply kept the slip of paper and didn't allow her to see it. He didn't even allow her to leave the tip on the table. It was both annoying and endearing. She couldn't remember how long it had been since a handsome man had bought her a meal. Was this a date? No. But this chance encounter felt special because Ezra was treating.

As they were leaving the restaurant, Ezra turned to her. He was so tall. She'd forgotten that, but she grew to appreciate it now. As a bear shifter female, she wasn't exactly built on the petite side, but Ezra made her feel that way. Oddly, it was a nice feeling.

"Since we're both headed in the same direction, do you want to ride together the rest of the way?" he asked, making her breath catch.

She hadn't ever imagined she'd meet up with him again, and now, here he was, wanting to travel the miles left before they reached their destination together. She couldn't find it within herself to refuse. Ezra was a good man. She knew that already. And it felt like he was still looking out for her.

She smiled at him. "Yeah. I'd like that."

He nodded then looked away. They agreed to make a final pit stop in the restrooms and meet out by the bikes. He informed her that she'd parked right next to him, and she had to admit to a little shivery feeling down her spine. It felt like fate had pushed her to this place... To this man, maybe?

She wasn't sure, but she was already looking forward to spending a little more time with him. Ezra Tate just made her feel safe. And that was something she hadn't felt in a very long time.

CHAPTER THREE

Ezra couldn't believe he was riding next to Thea. Meeting her again was really something, and the fact that she wanted to travel with him and had recovered so well from her ordeal made him feel...odd. His heart felt like it was expanding, letting the universe in to do a little tap dance of happiness, leaving him forever changed. For the better.

It was an expansive feeling. Something he couldn't really define, but it was good. Oh, so good.

They couldn't talk as they rode along at highway speeds, of course, but just knowing she was there, next to him, was something special. It was like she brought an energy with her that had been lacking in his life ever since she'd flown away with her folks all those weeks ago.

His inner bear had mourned her loss. He'd felt protective of her in a way he'd never really experienced before. He'd thought maybe it was just the circumstances of her rescue and the horrific conditions he'd found her in, but now, he wasn't so sure.

If it had just been the heat of the moment driving his emotions higher, they would have subsided in the intervening time, no? He was no expert, but he thought maybe seeing Thea now—recovered and riding a badass hog like she'd been born to it—would have cured him of any lingering feelings, if that had been all there was to it.

In a way, seeing her like this, so wild and free, made his heart feel good. As if rough patches had been healed, just knowing she was getting better and was already well enough to forge a new path for herself. In another way, the concern and protectiveness was still there. It had even ramped up a bit, if he was being honest with himself.

Knowing she was heading for the craziness of the rally made his bear want to roar. He *had to* watch over her. His inner bear wouldn't settle for anything less. The protectiveness had come full circle to a point where he couldn't let her go off on her own.

He knew, if she wanted to do her own thing in town, he'd be dogging her steps, watching out for her from afar, if he had to. He just knew he couldn't leave her on her own to fend for herself, no matter if she was on some kind of mystic vision quest or not.

He hadn't pulled her out of that basement prison only to let her fall prey to the first shady character that crossed her path. He was proud of her for wanting to go on an adventure after all she'd been through. That spoke volumes about her strength of character, as far as he was concerned. But, by the same token, he didn't like the risk her choices might expose her to, and he made a decision, then and there, that he'd be watching over her, whether she knew about it or not. He'd watch from the shadows if he had to, but he was going to make damned sure she was safe.

How exactly he was going to go about that while still completing his own mission, he wasn't sure, but he'd figure it out. Somehow. There was no other choice.

They stopped a few of times on their way in, but there was really no time or privacy to talk about anything important. As they drew closer to the place where all the motorcycles were heading, the number of bikes and people on the road increased until they were just one of many, all heading to the same destination.

There was a surprising camaraderie with the bikers they rubbed elbows with at the rest stops. The party atmosphere was already beginning, and the sheer number and variety of bikes on the road was impressive.

Ezra was going to enjoy his first trip to this part of the word—as long as he could stop the drug runners and keep Thea safe while she continued on her journey of self-exploration. He'd had more difficult missions in the past, but he was definitely setting himself up for a challenge. Good thing he excelled at meeting challenges. He'd make it work. He had no other choice.

When they rolled into town, hours later, Ezra led Thea straight to the hotel at which he'd reserved a suite. It was on the outskirts of town, away from all the commotion, for the most part. He led her inside and didn't give her a chance to object as he collected two keys to his room and gave her one.

He wouldn't do that for just anyone. In fact, it was very out of character for him to even consider sharing his space, or giving someone free access to his territory, albeit temporary territory.

It was still his den for the time he was there, and he usually wouldn't go handing out keys willy-nilly. That he didn't think twice about it in Thea's case said something. Something he'd have to think about at length.

For now, it was enough to know she'd have a place to run to if she needed it. Or a place just to lay her head if she needed rest.

It wasn't that long ago that she'd been so weak she'd been barely able to move. The busy town might get to her. In which case, he hoped she'd take advantage of that key and come here to find some peace.

"This is nice," Thea said as she walked into the suite.

There were two bedrooms with a bathroom between them—the kind with two doors, one from each of the bedrooms. The door opened into the main room, which was set up like a living room in a house with a couch, coffee table and conversation area on one side, a dining room table and chairs on the other, with a small kitchenette along the far wall. There was a fridge, cooktop, microwave, sink and a few cabinets with supplies.

"As you can see, there's plenty of room. I don't need all this space," Ezra assured her.

"So, why did you rent a suite, then?" she asked, turning on him with a suspicious lift to her eyebrow.

"Short notice. It was all I could get, and to be honest, I like the buffer of space between me and the neighbors. You know how territorial we can be," he said quietly, not needing to elaborate further. She was, after all, also a bear shifter.

She nodded. "Yeah, I can see that. But won't you mind sharing the territory, such as it is, with me?"

"Oddly enough, no," he answered honestly. "Probably because of the way we met, you rouse all sorts of protective instincts in me, but it's not just that. You feel...comfortable. Kind of soothing to my other half, in a way." He lifted his shoulders, unsure how to put the feeling into words but wanting to be as open as he could with her.

She'd frowned when he'd brought up their first encounter, but the look faded to one of curiosity as he elaborated. Good. He didn't want her to think he only wanted her around because he had seen her at her most vulnerable and wanted to protect her. Bear shifter females—any strong female—usually didn't take well to that sort of thing, in his experience.

And he didn't want that for her, either. He wanted her to be strong. To stand on her own two feet in any relationship—whether it be just friendship or...something more. At this point, he had to admit, he was *very* interested in pursuing that *something more* with her.

"Don't take this the wrong way, but I feel some of that, too. My other half feels comfortable around you," she admitted, seeming almost shy about her words. "That isn't something I feel around men since..."

He nodded sadly. "I understand. I want you to know that,

no matter what, you're safe with me, Thea. I won't let anything bad happen to you again. Ever."

Her eyes brightened with tears she didn't let fall, nodding as she took a moment to regain her composure. "I feel that, with you, Ezra. I mean… I'm strong now. Stronger than I was even before Bolivar. That experience changed me in ways I'm only just beginning to understand, but you've remained constant. Running into you on the highway… It was like nothing had changed. Not in a bad way. I mean, I've changed, but *you* haven't. And that's a really good thing." She leaned back against the top of the sofa and shook her head. "I'm not making much sense, am I?" Her smile softened her words, and he found himself smiling along with her.

"It's okay. I think I understand," he told her in a gentle tone of voice as he moved closer.

He wanted so much to touch her. To take her into his arms and give her a bear hug. But not just yet. He knew it was too soon. She'd been through so much. He didn't want to scare her off by being too grabby.

Instead, he reached down and took hold of the saddlebags she held loosely in one hand. He met her eyes, and they were close…closer than he'd anticipated. The question in her gaze turned to something much warmer, but he kept his resolve. He wouldn't try anything physical with her unless and until he knew for certain it wouldn't send her running away from him. Her safety was too important. More important than his own selfish desires.

She relinquished the saddlebags to him, and he straightened, moving slightly away. Out of the danger zone before he did something he couldn't take back.

"Which bedroom do you want?" he asked. "I think they're both basically the same. Right or left?"

She got up from her leaning position and went ahead of him to scout the rooms. One was a little more femininely decorated than the other, so she wisely chose that one. Though, to be fair, he didn't really care one way or the other what color paint was on the walls, as this was only a temporary place to hang his hat.

He dropped her saddlebags on the chair near the dresser and left her to settle in. He'd left his own bags in the main room, so he retrieved them and headed for the other bedroom.

He took off his jacket, checked his messages and heard the water running in the bathroom between the two bedrooms. Good. She was settling in.

The bear within him wanted to rumble in satisfaction. She was here, in his territory, and she'd agreed to stay. All was well with the world. At least for the moment.

Ezra had found messages waiting for him on his phone, which he hadn't checked since the last rest stop on the road. His crew for this job was in town and ready for a meet, though Ace recommended waiting until tomorrow, so they could arrange some sort of casual encounter. Ezra spent a few minutes texting back and forth, and the plan was set.

He was free for the rest of the night, and he hoped he could spend that time with Thea. They were both a little beat from the trip, so he assumed she'd probably like to have a relatively quiet night to recuperate. He'd take her to dinner— or order dinner in, if she really wasn't up to going out again.

From the sound of water in the pipes, he suspected Thea was taking a shower. He checked his own road-dust spattered appearance and realized he could do with a bit of a cleanup himself.

Ezra spent the next few minutes making himself more presentable and then made himself leave the bedroom. The audible swish of water was making him think lusty thoughts and the last thing she needed was some hard-luck bear with a boner sniffing after her right now.

Ezra forced his libido back down and opened his laptop. He sat out at the table in the main room and studied the paper trail he had compiled while he waited for Thea to make a reappearance. Luckily, the reminder of why he was here and what was at stake did the trick, and he was soon lost in the money trail that led to Zappo's Bike Repair on the edge of town.

Thea felt about a thousand times better after her shower. She emerged from the bedroom she'd chosen to find Ezra staring at a small computer screen while tapping the keys more rapidly than she ever would have expected. He knew how to type. Like for real. All fingers on the right keys and everything.

"I'm impressed," she told him, moving to stand near the table but angled so she couldn't read his screen, giving him a bit of privacy for his work.

"By what?" he said, looking up and then stretching, as if he'd been deep into work for a while. She'd been in the shower, and then in her bedroom, for a lot longer than she'd thought, so it was possible he'd been working all that time.

"You can type," she said quickly, trying hard not to notice the way his muscles moved as he stretched his arms above his head. Ezra was a handsome man, and in just a T-shirt and jeans, he was mouth-wateringly tempting.

He glanced back at his laptop. "Yeah, I learned back when I was in school. Saved me a lot of hassle and headache knowing the right way to get the best use out of a keyboard all these years."

"I just can't picture you sitting behind a desk all day," she told him, scrunching up her nose as she tried to imagine it. Nope. Didn't work.

"Well, I don't do it *all* day," he allowed, shutting down his laptop and closing the screen. "But a lot of my work involves research. These days, that means logging time on the net." He stood from the table then picked up his laptop in one beefy hand. "What do you want to do for dinner? Go out to a restaurant or order something in?"

She tilted her head to one side, thinking. Going out in public might be safer.

If she stayed here with him, the mood might get a little too intimate. She was very much afraid she'd crawl into his arms and never want to leave.

Where were these thoughts coming from? He was her savior, after all, but over the past few hours in his company, new desires had risen with more power than she had expected.

She'd thought almost from the first moment she'd seen him, back in that hellish basement, that he was attractive, but now, there was a new awareness awakening. A new yearning that was growing.

Dangerous stuff. Especially for a woman who wasn't really sure who she was anymore.

Did Ezra even want to feel anything for her other than the protectiveness he'd admitted to earlier? Best she didn't stir up too much trouble for now.

"Let's go out. I didn't really see too much of the town yet, and I'd like to get acclimated a little more," she told him. It sounded reasonable. Sensible, even. She wouldn't admit to the fact that he was just too darn sexy for her frame of mind right now.

"All right. Give me a minute to get my jacket, and we can go. I understand there's a really good restaurant a brisk walk from here, if you don't mind going on foot. I figured you might want a chance to stretch your legs after all the riding we did today."

Thoughtful as well as kind. Damn. Ezra just kept becoming more attractive the more they were together. She'd have to be really cautious around him, not to lose her head...or her heart.

Dinner was delicious, even if the setting was a bit more raucous than Thea had expected. The restaurant also had a large bar along one wall of the large room.

A half-wall topped with metal poles and frosted glass panels separated the two areas, but the bar was so full, people were spilling over. The waitstaff didn't seem to mind, allowing bar patrons to sit at the restaurant side tables as long as they allowed the waiters and waitresses to fetch their drinks and ordered some snacks.

Thea and Ezra were seated closer to the bar than she probably would have liked, but the festive atmosphere felt friendly rather than threatening. And, she was with Ezra. Nothing would harm her while he was here. She knew that for a fact.

So, when three big guys stopped in front of their table, she wasn't too worried. Her nose told her right away that these three were shifters. Even with all the various scents in the room, she smelled the distinct tang of fur. Bear fur.

"Will you look what the cat dragged in?" the man in the center of the trio said, grinning widely. "How you doing, Ez? And who is this lovely lady? Surely, she's not with you?"

Ezra stood to shake each of the men's hands in turn. "Good to see you, Ace. Jack. King."

Thea's eyebrows rose at the odd names.

"Our parents worked the casinos in Reno," the youngest-looking of the three told her with a wink.

"This is Thea," Ezra introduced her. "Thea, these three are old friends, and the best damned mechanics I've ever known."

Thea nodded to each man in turn. If Ezra was describing them as friends, then they were all right. Ezra would be giving off more dangerous vibes if they weren't. As it was, he was calm and steady, making her feel the same. Her inner bear was very sensitive and had pretty much aligned her instincts to his moods over the past few hours. That, in itself, was a little freaky, if she'd given herself the chance to stop and think about it.

"Would you like to join us?" Thea asked politely, looking at Ezra to see if he approved.

Ace made a show of looking over the crowded bar area and then back at the big table they'd been given. "If you're sure you don't mind," he said, glancing at her before turning his full attention to Ezra.

Ezra held out an open hand in a welcoming gesture. "Pull up a chair," he told the men. "I was going to look you up tomorrow, anyway, to take a look at my bike. I'm having an engine issue that I can't pin down and was hoping you could help with."

That was news to Thea. She'd been riding with him all day, and his engine had sounded fine. Maybe there was more to this meeting than she'd thought? She knew Ezra was in town to do some troubleshooting. Maybe these guys had something to do with his job.

They spent the next hour talking with the three brothers about motorcycles, the rally, the town and the shop they were working out of for rally week. Apparently, they were normally based out of Phoenix but had signed on for seasonal work during the rally at a well-known shop on the edge of town.

Eventually, as the noise level from the bar rose and the night wore on, Ezra and Thea got up to leave. The brothers stayed, with promises to look at Ezra's bike tomorrow.

Ezra and Thea walked back to the hotel in silence, enjoying the crisp night air. The only thing that would have been better was if she'd been able to let her bear out for a walk around in the cold dark, but there were way too many humans around. Way too many guns and too much alcohol, which was always a bad combination. She would have to be content to walk on two feet tonight…and probably for the remainder of her stay in this town.

When they reached his suite at the hotel, Ezra spent a few minutes prowling around, sniffing everything. Then, he brought out an electronic gizmo from his pocket and went over the room with it, finally putting it away with a satisfied grunt.

"We can talk freely here. Nobody's been in here since we left, and there's no electronic surveillance, though that could change. I'll alert you if it does, but I don't expect it, honestly. It's just always good to check," he told her.

Thea was curious about his preparedness for detecting listening devices but chose to ask about something else instead. "Those three men at the restaurant… Are they helping you with your job here?"

He looked at her with surprise clear on his face. "How could you tell?"

"I'm not really sure. It was just a feeling," she admitted.

He relaxed a bit. "Well, then, you have good instincts." He went to the conversation area and waited for Thea to be seated before lowering himself onto the overstuffed couch next to her, but far enough away to give her a bit of space. "The brothers are here to do a little surveillance for me and to act as backup. They really are mechanics. We'd arranged to meet tomorrow, but running into them at the restaurant was actually better."

"You hadn't planned that?" she asked, curious.

"No. They had no way of knowing we'd be there. I just figured I'd bring my bike into their temporary place of employment tomorrow," he told her. "The shop they're working out of this week is owned by my employers, though it's just one of many businesses in their portfolio."

"The one you suspect is being used to smuggle drugs, right?" she asked, remembering their earlier conversation.

Ezra nodded. "Yeah, they're going to be my inside men since it wouldn't be easy for me to get the proof I need otherwise. If and when there's a confrontation with the current manager and employees, the brothers will act as my backup, if needed."

"Are they members of your Clan?" Thea asked. Bears didn't have huge Clans, but it was possible the bonds between Ezra and the three brothers went deep.

"No," he answered quickly, but with no particular emphasis. "I'm kind of a loner. I've been skipping around from place to place since I got out of the military, so aside from my folks, I don't really claim a Clan anywhere, though I do work for Trevor and Beth, and they're part of the group out of Grizzly Cove. Trev's been trying to convince me to put down roots there."

"I've heard a little bit about it," Thea observed. "They put out a call for female bear shifters a while back, right?"

"Yeah," Ezra admitted with a chuckle. "Those guys have a

really grand vision for the town they're building. I thought it was crazy when I first heard about it, but they're actually making it work. The town is pretty nice, and they've gathered a lot of allies."

"I had some vague thoughts about visiting there on my way home," she revealed. Not that she was really *looking* for a mate... But the idea of a group of male bear shifters starting their own community was intriguing.

"If you want to see the town, I'd be happy to show you around," he offered, surprising her.

"You'll probably be sick of having me around long before then," she joked, feeling a little melancholy even just saying the words. She liked being around him. Perhaps a bit too much.

"I seriously doubt that could ever happen," he replied, both his gaze and his voice more serious than she'd expected.

He'd moved closer to her on the couch while they'd been talking, but she hadn't really noticed until now that she'd moved nearer to him, too. There wasn't a whole lot of room separating them right now, in fact. When he moved his arm from being draped over the back of the sofa to just lightly touching her shoulder, she felt the intimacy of their nearness and wanted to be closer still.

"I like having you around, Thea," he went on, his tone deep and a little bit growly. The sound went right through her, to stroke the core of her being like a warm, velvet touch. She liked the sensation and wanted more.

But was this wise? The little voice in the back of her head wanted to stop and examine things, but the larger part of her heart didn't give a damn. She liked being near Ezra, and that's all that really mattered in that moment.

She moved, of her own volition, into his arms, pressing herself against him. Oh, she remembered that feeling. Ezra's strong embrace.

She'd dreamed about the way he'd held her during those terrible times just after he and his friends had rescued her from that prison. She thought she'd been imagining the safety she'd felt, but no. Ezra was just as she remembered him. Strong, secure and protective.

He also smelled…perfect. Like her inner bear's idea of the perfect man.

The bear was already half in love with him. Her bear had been so badly damaged by Bolivar and the terrible blood magic he'd been working on her soul. Ezra had put a stop to that, and his strength had given her the ability to come back even stronger. He'd almost coaxed her bear back into being, if that was even possible, when the poor thing had almost given up the ghost.

As a result, her inner bear was loyal to him even now, but it felt like more than just that. It felt like he could be important to her. *Very* important.

Ezra stroked his hands down Thea's back, making sure his touch was as gentle as he could make it. He hadn't expected her to want to be so close to him. At least not so quickly.

He didn't want to do anything that might scare her off, but just having her in his arms again was making him feel things that might get him into trouble.

His instincts were roaring to life inside him, wanting him to claim her in some way. To put his mark on her—not in a hurtful way, but in a way that would let her know of his interest in no uncertain terms.

But would that drive her away? If he kissed her now, would she run screaming into the night? Would it be a betrayal of the trust she was giving him at this very moment?

Ezra didn't know what to do. That was unusual for a bear of his age and experience. He wasn't used to being so unsure of his next move.

Good thing Thea appeared not to have the same problem. When she raised her head and looked deep into his eyes, he thought he was going to die if he didn't kiss her within the next five seconds.

And then, she kissed him.

Glory be to the Mother of All.

CHAPTER FOUR

Thea didn't know where she'd gotten the nerve, but she didn't regret whatever impulse had driven her to kiss him. After just the slightest hesitation, he had taken control of the kiss and proven to her that the attraction wasn't all one-sided. He kissed her like he'd been dreaming about it as long as she had.

She didn't know what gave her that idea, but her inner bear approved of his enthusiasm and the delicious sensations he was causing in her body. It had been so long since she'd felt like a desirable woman. Since her kidnapping, she hadn't dared go out on a date. Not even with a human man.

Her bear was a lot stronger than she'd ever been now, which gave Thea more confidence about being able to defend herself, but she hadn't wanted to meet any new men. She hadn't wanted to make the effort to find a companion, even though her inner bear had been driving her pretty hard to look for a mate before her ordeal.

It was as if the bear had learned patience. Or, maybe... Maybe she'd decided that Ezra was someone she'd like to meet again someday. He'd made a very strong impression on both sides of her nature, and though she hadn't been sure they would ever meet again, she had been sort of subconsciously comparing all the men she knew to him ever since she'd gone back home.

Taking off on her adventure had been at least partially about cleansing her mind of the one man who seemed to have taken over her thoughts. And then, she'd run into him on the road. A random thing that had all the markings of the hand of the Goddess, or Fate, the Universe, or whatever, playing with her life in what she hoped would turn out to be a positive way.

Judging by the sensations Ezra's kiss evoked in her body, and the sexy way he was growling, the interaction was *very* positive already. He reclined, taking her with him so that she was draped over him like a blanket. Mmm. That felt really good. He was warm and hard in all the right places.

Very hard in one particular place that made her blush just thinking about it. Not that she objected. Nope. Not at all.

She took over control of the kiss at that point, wanting to get closer to him, but then, she became aware of a distant ringing. Ezra's hands stopped where they were, midway down her back, and she stilled. What was that noise, and how dare it interrupt them? She lifted her lips from his, confused.

"Sorry, honey." He seemed embarrassed and annoyed in equal measure. "I've got to get that."

She sat up, and he did the same. "What is it?"

The tinkling noise came again, and she realized it was his phone. As he dug it out of his pocket, the melody became clearer. It was the tune to "I Shot the Sheriff". Somebody had a custom ringtone, and she wondered who it was.

"It's a friend from Grizzly Cove. The sheriff, to be precise," he told her with a hint of a smile. "He doesn't often call me, so it's got to be important. Sorry." He apologized again as he stood, heading for his bedroom to take the call.

Thea tried to calm her breathing and gather her wits. What had just happened here? Had she totally lost her mind?

She ought to feel a little embarrassed at how easily she

went from seeking comfort to demanding pleasure, but she couldn't find it within herself to regret what had just happened. That was significant. Her inner bear wasn't protesting her actions, but rather the loss of Ezra's warmth and the pleasure he had brought her. Interesting.

She could hear the low rumble of his voice in the other room. She wasn't trying to eavesdrop, but her hearing was good. He knew just how good, so if he wasn't taking further precautions against being overheard—like going into the bathroom and running the shower or something—then he probably didn't mind if she heard his side of the conversation. Even she couldn't hear the other end of the line from the other room, so perhaps he'd gone into the bedroom because he didn't know what the man on the other end would have to say and whether or not she should hear it.

Made sense, even if she was feeling unreasonable about the loss of his warmth. His kiss. She'd really been enjoying their embrace. She'd loved the feel of him against her and the way he made her senses come alive. He tasted like warm honey on a hot summer day—something her bear side thought of as the highest possible compliment.

He just took her breath away on every level.

Getting up from the couch, she headed for her bedroom. The kiss had been monumental, but it would be awkward to pick up from where they'd left off. Better to save the awkward moment for the morning, when she wasn't feeling quite so vulnerable.

If she was being logical about this, she'd gone about as far as she was prepared to go for the first day of their reunion. If they'd continued down the path to ultimate pleasure, she wasn't totally sure that either of them wouldn't be facing regrets the next morning. Better to slow things down a bit. They'd made good progress today and ended on a good note.

Tomorrow was another day…and another opportunity to get into his pants. If that's what they both wanted in the harsh light of day. She chuckled as she closed her bedroom door. He was still on the phone, but he'd figure out she was done for the day. It was just better this way. At least, for now.

The next morning, Ezra was up well before Thea. He listened at her door for a moment, hearing the steady breathing that told him she was still sound asleep. They'd had a long day yesterday, and he was happy enough to let her sleep in.

He left a note on the table in case she woke while he was gone, then he headed out on a supply mission. He picked up groceries for the refrigerator—particularly breakfast ingredients—then worked his way back to the room. Thea was still asleep when he returned, so he started cooking breakfast. He was hungry, and he figured she'd come out if the scent of cooking bacon had the same power over her that it did him.

He grinned as he set the pan of bacon on the cooktop. Sure enough, about fifteen minutes later, Thea's door opened. She looked adorably rumpled, her hair a little messy and her eyes a little heavy-lidded. She looked cute. Like a sleepy mama bear just coming out of hibernation.

"You got bacon?" The final word sounded like she was referring to the Holy Grail or some other sacred object.

"Bacon, eggs, bread for toast, and some other stuff. I figured if we're going to be here a few days, we might as well stock the fridge," he told her. She shuffled into the kitchen area to look over his shoulder at the nearly-done pan full of bacon, inhaling with a sappy smile on her face.

"Can I help cook?" she asked, her gaze never leaving the crispy bacon in the pan.

"Not today. I've got it. Why don't you set the table, and I'll serve this up? Do you want eggs?" He began taking the bacon out of the frying pan and placing it on the paper-lined plate he'd prepared to help blot up some of the grease.

"Yes, please. Can I have two, scrambled well?" she asked in a prim voice, still eyeing the bacon.

"Coming right up. You want toast with that?" As he said the words, the toaster popped, and two perfectly browned slices came into view.

"I'll take those, if you don't mind," she told him, reaching for the fresh toast.

She politely reloaded the toaster with two new slices and set it to toast before heading to the table. She'd set out plates while they'd been talking, and Ezra followed her, placing the plate of bacon in the center of the table.

"Start on that, and I'll have your eggs ready in a few minutes," he told her, feeling indulgent because his inner bear liked providing for her. It made him feel all warm and fuzzy inside.

He made her eggs and his all at the same time, dividing up the mound in the frying pan and giving her the smaller portion. He took his seat at the table after serving them both and noticed the bacon sandwich she'd made with her toast and half the plate of bacon. It seemed like she'd been very deliberate about leaving exactly half of the bacon for him, which was sweet, but he wouldn't have minded if she'd eaten the whole thing. He wanted her to have whatever she wanted—even if that meant he'd have to make more bacon for himself.

The thought struck him as he broke up the crunchy bacon into his eggs. He would happily go without so that she had what she wanted. He'd never really felt that way about any other female who wasn't related to him. That probably meant something important, but as he started to think through the possibilities—all of them intriguing in a scary sort of way—his phone started singing out with alerts for incoming text messages. Three or four in a row.

He reached for his phone and placed it on the table next to his plate. "Sorry. It sounds like someone wants to get in touch with me pretty badly."

"No problem. I don't mind," she told him, busying herself with her eggs as he scanned the incoming messages.

"Damn," Ezra mumbled, reading the urgent texts from Ace, who was at the bike shop, and his brother, Jack, who was on the other side of town. It was a three-way text. "Thea,

I hate to say this, but you should probably stay inside today."

"What? Why?" she wanted to know.

"Someone is stirring up trouble between the groups of shifters in town this week. There are at least three werewolf Packs, plus a few more bears, besides us five. Apparently, they're talking about some sort of blood feud, but the reasons aren't clear." He tapped out a brief answer on his phone and sent it on its way. "I'm going to have to check this out," he told her, standing. "I'm sorry to leave like this in the middle of breakfast, but I need to know what's happening, and if all-out war can be prevented. Jack seems to think there's something funny about the way this is developing. He has a nose for magic, and he said…" Damn, this was going to be hard to say to her, of all people. "He said there might be a magical component to this. He thinks someone is driving the violence."

Her face drained of color, and she dropped her fork. "There's a mage here, manipulating the shifter population into fighting?"

"It's possible," he told her, though Jack had said it was the likely situation.

"Then, I'm coming with you," she said, shocking the hell out of him as she stood.

"Say what?" He rocked back on his heels, unprepared for her fierce stance.

"I refuse to cower from some bastard mage who thinks he can maneuver us into bleeding for his perversions. I'll help you track him down and kill the bastard."

Wow. She was serious. Mama bear was riled up, and no way did Ezra have the heart to tell her she couldn't come with him. She deserved a chance to get a little of her own back. She had earned the right to stand on her own two feet and face down a danger like the one that had trapped her before. She probably needed to know she could, as a further step in her recovery.

But this time, Ezra would be standing right behind her, backing her up. He'd let her do her thing, but if she needed help at any point, he was there to let her know she wasn't alone.

"All right," he said, finally, coming to a decision. "Dress in your leathers. We're going to be among bikers. Shifters, too. But they're all different breeds connected by their love of bikes. We need to fit in."

"So long as they figure out I'm the Alpha bitch in charge, we're all going to get along fine." A steely look entered her eyes before she spun and headed for her bedroom. Ezra finished shoveling the rest of his breakfast into his mouth. He was already dressed for action, but he'd wait for Thea. He liked this gutsy new side of her.

Thea went into her bedroom and lost a bit of the steam that had driven her to volunteer—no, demand—to go with Ezra. What was she thinking? Had she even *been* thinking when she'd made that demand?

She wasn't sure where all that bravado had come from, but in the moment, it had felt good. Really good. As if she was evolving into...someone she could be really proud of. No more hiding in the corner, locking herself away in her parents' home. She was wild and free and on her own for the first time in her life.

Well, not completely on her own. Having Ezra here was probably what was making her feel so bold. She had this sense that, no matter what kind of trouble she might find herself in, he'd be there to back her up.

She felt her bear demanding that she do the same for him. Equals. Alphas. Partners?

She wasn't sure where that thought was coming from either...only that it felt really, really *right*.

She dressed quickly, ready for action in just a few minutes. Shifters got good at dressing and undressing faster than most people, and their clothing was never fussy. Easy on, easy off, ready to shift into whatever form was best suited to the situation.

When she came out of the bedroom, shrugging into her

jacket, she found Ezra waiting for her. He handed her something that she took without question, only realizing a moment later what it was.

"I turned the rest of your breakfast into a sandwich. You can eat it on our way out the door," he told her.

A little piece of her heart melted at the sweet gesture. What a nice thing he'd done for her. Food was one of the most basic, most important things to a shifter. The fact that he'd thought enough about her welfare to make sure she got to finish her breakfast was very indicative of his protectiveness and generosity. How could anyone possibly not like this man? He was a big teddy bear.

They rolled into the bike shop a few minutes later. The sign above the garage bays proudly proclaimed they were arriving at Zappo's Bike Repair. The small garage had three open bays, but there were no hydraulic lifts in this shop. No, this place was strictly for vehicles of the two-wheeled variety.

There were bikes in various states of completion all over the place, and at least a half-dozen guys working on them throughout the three bays. There were another three guys in the office, dithering over parts. Every single one of them looked up when Thea got off her bike. She sniffed delicately. In addition to the bear brothers they'd met last night, there were a whole lot of wolves present. And they were all watching the sway of her hips as she walked toward Ezra.

Thank goodness, he'd waited politely for her to join him. She would not feel entirely comfortable facing down a dozen lusty shifters all by herself, but then again—they were wolves. Her bear would eat them for breakfast if they tried any shit with her. Grrr.

She didn't know where this new feistiness had come from, but she liked it. Prior to her abduction, she'd never really been a forceful woman. Now, the bear had really come out to play, asserting itself even while she was in human form, probably to protect her better than it had in the past. No way was Thea going to be an easy mark now or in the future. If someone wanted to hurt her…well…they could try, but she'd put up one hell of a fight, and anyone who dared touch her without permission would get bloody—by her claws. That was for certain.

Ezra held out an elbow, and she slid her arm through his, making a clear statement that they were together. The change in the speculative feel of the looks sent her way was welcome. She'd just gone from being available to claimed, and as caveman-ish as that was, in shifter culture, that meant only an idiot who wanted to tangle with Ezra would try anything with Thea. He had very clearly just put her under his protection. The big lug, she thought affectionately. He really was the sweetest man.

Ezra escorted her directly into the bay where two of the bear brothers she'd met last night were working. When they saw her, both of them wiped off their hands on nearby rags and came forward to give her hugs in greeting, one at a time. It was a bear thing. Bear hugs were the best kind, after all.

After spending the previous evening with them, Thea felt comfortable with the brothers. Especially knowing that Ezra trusted them to get the inside scoop on this place. She looked around as she stood back and Ezra exchanged greetings with his operatives. Only Ace and King were there. Jack had been following a lead, if she recalled what Ezra had said before they left the hotel. Perhaps he was still out there, following it. In the meantime, there were a lot of eyes on Thea and Ezra, and from the scents, they were all werewolves. Very curious werewolves.

An older werewolf came out of the office and headed straight for them. Ace made a show of noticing the older man's interest and stepped forward to make the introductions.

"Boss, this is an old friend of mine and his lady friend. Ezra Tate and Thea Jackson. Guys, this is Francis Benito, manager of this establishment." Thea watched as the two Alpha males—albeit of different species—sized each other up. Finally, the older man stuck out his hand.

"Friends call me Frank," he said in a voice that sounded

like it had been honed with sandpaper.

"Frank," Ezra said politely. "Nice place you got here." Ezra made a show of looking all around the repair bays at the bikes in various states of repair.

"Nice wheels," Frank said, nodding toward Ezra's vintage motorcycle.

From there, the two men launched into a conversation filled with numbers and model names. Real gear-head talk that Thea really couldn't follow. She'd bought her bike because Margo—the werewolf woman who had been a big part of Thea's rescue—had ridden a Harley. Margo was badass, and Thea remembered looking at the other woman and wanting to be more like her. Alpha. In control. Able to take care of herself and drive a big, scary machine.

Thea had come to love her new bike in the weeks since she'd purchased it and learned how to ride. She wasn't quite in Ezra's class when it came to being knowledgeable about the machine, but she was learning as she went along. She wasn't sure she'd ever become an aficionado, though. She was capable but didn't have a lot of experience with mechanical things. She could fix something in a pinch, but she didn't know all the inner workings of bikes the way the men around her right now did. It just wasn't something that interested her.

She'd much rather feel the wind against her body, buffeting her as she rode along than spend much time thinking about the gears and pistons that made everything work. She also liked the functional fashion that went along with riding. Leather was awesome to wear. It made her feel sexy. Judging by the attention she'd been getting from males of every species along her journey so far, she looked good in it, too. That boosted her confidence, which was a good feeling.

As Ezra moved away with Frank to discuss his vintage bike, Thea realized Ace and King were flanking her, one on either side. One held some kind of wrench in his hand. The other was still wiping grease off his fingers with a rag. She glanced at each of them in turn, but they were watching everything but her. It was like they were guarding her or something. For a moment, Thea felt a little bit like royalty with her very own honor guard.

The sound of an approaching motor broke that daydream. She recognized the man on the big machine. It was the missing brother of the trio, Jack. After parking his own bike, he came right up to her and gave her a bear hug in greeting. Of the three, Jack had the liveliest personality.

He took her hands in his after the hug and looked into her eyes. "You all right?"

How did Jack know...? Damn. Ezra must have told the brothers something about how they'd met.

Thea gently disengaged her hands from his—a statement of her own strength. "I'm fine. Hoping to kick some ass, but otherwise fine."

A wolf who was loitering just a little too close behind them chuckled, and she turned to look at him. Something about him seemed a little off, but they'd come here to gather information, and it looked like this guy wanted to speak.

"You know where I can do a little of that ass kicking?" Thea asked the young werewolf bluntly. Bears weren't known for the subtlety, so she figured it was okay to come out and say something like that to him, considering what he'd just overheard her saying.

He chuckled again in a way that sent shivers of alarm down her spine. Something was not right with this boy.

"Yeah. Gonna have a brawl at the full moon. Gonna kill some of those White Oaks pussies." If he'd been in wolf form, the young man would have been drooling. Damn. The look in his glassy eyes was downright creepy.

"What is White Oaks?" Thea asked.

"A Pack that rolled into town from Iowa. They come every year for the rally," another of the mechanic wolves nearby answered. He seemed a little less...*wrong*...than the younger man, but there was still something off about his eyes. "They're going to learn they should just stay home and out of our territory next year. If any of them are still alive after tomorrow night."

The conversation came to a halt as Ezra and Frank returned. The younger wolves went back to work on their respective projects while the bear brothers surrounded Thea protectively and sent each other speculative looks. They had all seemed surprised by the answers to Thea's questions, and she wondered if she'd just elicited more information from their co-workers in three minutes than they had in three days.

The thought was enough to make her smile. Ezra returned her smile as he walked right up to her and put his arm around her waist. The others moved off to give him room, and Frank left with an abstract wave for them both. He went back into his office and didn't come out again.

"Seen enough?" she asked Ezra, as if she'd had enough of the motorcycle shop and just wanted to go and have fun somewhere else. She could play the demanding girlfriend if she had to.

"Yeah, for now, I guess." Ezra's tone made it sound like he was giving in to her, but he made sure to turn back to the other bears. "Can we talk more about the mods later?"

"Sure thing. We're in town all week," King told Ezra.

"I was hoping we could discuss it later today. You guys take a lunch break?" Ezra asked with the just right amount of casualness, Thea thought.

"Yeah, we usually get burgers over at Molloy's," Jack piped up. "You and your lady are welcome to join us. Not many of our kind here this year, and I haven't seen such a pretty female in a long time," was Jack's comment as he gave Thea a good-natured leer.

She laughed at his over-the-top flirting and looked at Ezra, but he was cool. It was pretty clear that Jack was only being friendly and wasn't trying to steal Thea away from Ezra in any way. Bears were playful sometimes, and Jack seemed to be that kind of personality. Thea found him charming in a brotherly sort of way.

"We'll see you there," Ezra told the men. "Lunch is on me."

"Then, we'll definitely see you there," Ace replied, grinning. He reached forward to shake Ezra's hand in farewell, and Ezra repeated the gesture with each of the other brothers before turning to go.

CHAPTER FIVE

Thea followed Ezra as they got on their bikes and headed away from the garage. Once they were out of sight, he gestured for her to pull over into the large parking lot of a strip mall. She followed him to a corner of the lot where they parked their bikes and shut down the motors so they could talk quietly.

"Sorry about that," Ezra said first, before she could ask him what that little encounter had all been about. "There were way too many wolves there to discuss anything, and they all smelled off to me."

"Off how?" she asked, instead of the many other things running through her mind.

"I don't know." He grimaced and shook his head once. "It could be drugs, but most shifters don't bother with that stuff. I didn't think there were any human drugs that could really affect our kind to any large degree—unless they took massive quantities. Our metabolisms are just too fast-burning to let the effect last very long."

"Do you think there's something new on the market?" Thea grew concerned. Maybe it wasn't magic that was screwing with those wolves, but something man-made.

"I'm not sure. It seems improbable." Ezra shook his head again. "Or, it could be what Jack mentioned on the phone."

"Magic." Thea felt dread settle in the pit of her stomach.

"Yeah." Ezra sighed and looked away. "I'm really sorry, Thea. This is the last thing I wanted to involve you in."

"Yeah, but if it's affecting shifters in this town, and I'm here... Well, I'm going to be involved in it one way or another. I figure it's better to work with you to end the problem before it gets out of hand."

She was astonished to find she really did feel that way. She'd been concerned that fear would cripple her if she ever encountered a situation where magic was involved again, but she was surprising herself. She wasn't afraid. She was pissed. Her inner bear was angry and riled. She wanted to help solve the problem and eradicate the threat. She didn't feel in the least bit like running.

And that made her feel proud of herself. Even she hadn't been sure how she would react if she ever came up against evil magic again. Now, she knew. She could trust herself to fight back and not want to flee. As any self-respecting bear shifter should.

Ezra was looking at her. Studying her as if he was trying to figure out if there was more than just bravado behind her words. Either that or he was trying to gauge the strength of her resolve. Or a combination of both. He'd soon learn that she wasn't going to wimp out on him. No. That part of her life was over. Nobody was ever going to take her again without a fight. To the death, if necessary.

"Those wolves weren't right in the head," she went on when he didn't say anything further. "Did you see their eyes? Glassy. Like they were doped up...or under some kind of spell."

"The eyes were why I thought drugs," he said. "I've seen enough humans on drugs to know that glassy look, but this was slightly different. Can you tell if someone's been messed with magically just by looking at them?"

It was Thea's turn to shake her head, but she wasn't giving him a negative answer. No, she was just trying to banish the bad feelings that came with remembering her experience in Bolivar's basement of horrors.

"You can to some extent," she answered quietly, trying to gather her words and suppress her feelings at the same time. "Bolivar would sometimes bring in other mages. Not often and not many. I got the impression they were his superiors, and he was trying to impress them with his collection."

The shock on Ezra's face was total. She'd never spoken about the visitors to anyone, though she probably should have by this point in her recovery. For a long time, she hadn't remembered, and when the memories started returning as she grew stronger physically, she hadn't *wanted* to remember.

"Sweet Mother of All," Ezra whispered, holding his hand out to her then letting it drop as if he didn't know what to do or how to respond.

"The thing is, I don't think the other girls remember it. You see, Bolivar would do some sort of spell casting before he brought down his guests, but a lot of his magic bounced off me, which is why he was using me up first. I knew I would be the first to die of the women he was keeping captive. He was draining my power faster than the others. He drained us all—to keep us weak and pliable—but he was using me up first. He liked to bleed me, and each time, I felt another little part of my shifter soul slip away. It's taken a long time for me to get it back. My bear was almost gone when you saved me."

She reached out to him and took his big hand in her smaller one, squeezing tight. He seemed speechless, and she wanted to say what she had to say before she lost her nerve.

"When Bolivar brought his guests, the other girls would get a similar glassy-eyed look. They'd sit quietly while the visitors discussed us all like we were exhibits in a zoo. The other girls would even come when Bolivar called them, and say whatever he wanted them to say. It was disgusting and humiliating, and just so…wrong."

Ezra held her hand, and that little bit of his warmth helped her cope with the bad memories. He was such a strong man. He could banish the worst of her fears just by being there, with her.

"Is it the same look you saw just now in those men's eyes?" he asked gently.

She shuddered a little. "Yeah. It looked a lot like that," she admitted. "I think your friend Jack is right. If I had to bet, I'd say those wolves were under some sort of magical compulsion."

"Damn." Ezra looked away as if biting off a string of curse words in her presence, then he turned back to her. "I swear, I didn't know about any other mages, Thea. If I had, I would've been hunting them already. As it is, after this is over, I'll do what I can to make sure every last person who caused you grief in that hellhole will come to justice."

She squeezed his hand again and smiled softly at him. "It's not your fault. I don't think the other girls remember. I didn't remember it myself for a long time. It's only as my bear spirit came back to life and my body got stronger that everything started to come back, including those memories." She shrugged. "Maybe Bolivar's magic affected me more than I thought. Or, as weak as I was, his spells had more power over me than they normally would. I know I never fought when the visitors came. I just watched and hated. Silently. If I'd been stronger, I would've at least tried to claw them through the bars of my cage or something."

"You did what you needed to do to survive," he told her in a powerful tone that spoke directly to her bear. Alpha male to female needing reassurance. "You were smart, and you bided your time until help could come. There wasn't anything you could have done all on your own against Bolivar. He was too strong. Too cunning. And he had a gift of foresight that had allowed him to escape bigger groups and stronger shifters many times over several decades. The only reason we were able to get close enough was that we had a mage of our own whose powers foiled those of your captor."

"Gabe," she said softly. "I remember him from the mansion. He was nice. I hope he and Margo are doing okay."

"They're mated now," Ezra told her gently. Thea felt a surge of joy in her heart for the other couple.

"That's really great," she said, smiling. "They both really made an impression on me," she admitted. "I bought this bike because I wanted to be as badass as Margo. She was my role model for a while as I tried to regain my strength. I figured if a wolf shifter could be that tough, a bear should at least be able to do just as well."

"If not better," Ezra added, smiling back at her. "But I'll give Margo credit. She's more Alpha than most other Alpha wolves I've met, and that's saying something. Then again, Gabe is a power to be reckoned with, so they're a good match. I'm happy for them."

"Me, too," Thea added. "Maybe I can send them a mating gift," she thought aloud.

"I bet they'd like that," Ezra replied.

"So, what now?" She looked around, wondering where they'd go from here.

"Well, we've got a few hours to kill, so maybe we should do a little scouting and become a bit more familiar with the territory." They both knew the animal parts of their nature wouldn't settle until they'd scouted the perimeter and got to know the landmarks.

"Yeah, that sounds like a really good idea," Thea agreed.

They spent the next hours riding the perimeter of the town and getting to know the layout of its streets, then walking along some of the busier roads at the heart of town that had rows of shops. Even this early in the morning, there was a party atmosphere and many marquees set up along some streets sponsored by big corporations that ran the gamut from food to spirits and everything in between.

They scented a few other kinds of shifters in the crowd of more than half a million people that came into town just for this giant party every year, but no other bears. Maybe there were a few somewhere, but Ezra and Thea hadn't detected them so far on their tour of the town.

By the time lunch rolled around, they were more than ready to demolish a few burgers. Ezra opened the door to Molloy's Burger Bar for Thea, and the music inside spilled out onto the street. Although not too busy just yet, it was clear they were expecting a lunch rush and were well prepared.

Ezra stopped just inside the door to let his eyes adjust and spied Ace, King and Jack already seated at a large table in one corner. There were two open chairs and a pitcher of beer on the table that was already half empty. Ezra escorted Thea to the open spots, signaling to the approaching hostess that they'd found their party.

After greeting the brothers, they started looking at the menu, which consisted of several different types of hamburger. A waitress came over and took their orders, then they were left alone. Ezra had noted the position of the table, which the brothers must have chosen deliberately. They were in a corner, with empty tables on either side. They'd be able to talk in low tones and be relatively certain nobody could overhear—at least, until the place got more crowded and the nearby tables were filled.

Jack, sitting at the very corner of the table, between his two brothers and Ezra and Thea, who were on opposite sides, brought up the sensitive subject of magic. He spoke quietly, but Ezra and Thea could both hear his report clearly, though nobody else would. Not without special equipment, at any rate.

"There's definitely a mage here somewhere," Jack concluded when he'd finished outlining his movements and observations of the two major Packs of werewolves earlier in the day. "When I crossed paths with the White Oaks Alpha, I could feel some sort of magic rubbing my fur the wrong way. If he wasn't under some kind of compulsion, I'll eat my hat. And it's the same for the local Pack Alpha, when he came into the shop yesterday. There's something seriously wrong here, and somebody is getting their jollies pitting those two wolf Packs against each other."

"Well, thanks to Thea, we now know they're planning some sort of melee for tomorrow night's full moon. We just have to figure out where," Ace put in.

"But why maneuver wolves into fighting each other?" King asked, sounding puzzled.

"For their blood," Thea said, her voice sounding a little hollow to Ezra's ears. "Blood path mages get off on blood being spilled in violence. It gives them power. Makes them stronger."

"Son of a…" Ace swore and turned away.

"Are you sure about this?" King asked, his tone subdued.

"I've seen it before," Thea replied, her tone stronger, her delivery steadier. Ezra was proud of the way she was holding together, but he still hated the fact that she had to relive any part of what had happened to her in Lake Tahoe.

"You don't have to talk about this if you don't want to," Ezra told her softly.

"No. They need to know if we're going to stop this." She looked at the brothers. "I was held captive for a few months by a blood path mage. He bled me to steal my power and nearly killed my other half. Ezra saved my life."

The brothers were silent for a moment, as if in respect for what she'd been through, then Jack asked Ezra in a low voice. "How did you defeat the mage?"

Ezra frowned. "It wasn't my op." He looked away, as if in regret, then returned his focus to the men at the table. "I was backing up one of Colin Hastings' detectives, and she was partnered with a mage of incredible power. He was the one who took out the bastard who'd been holding Thea prisoner, along with several other women. Hastings called in strike teams and support from the Redstone Clan. It was a big op. We took out the human trafficking ring that the mage was helping in return for his pick of the women they abducted. He chose only the magical ones they caught in their net. Thea was the only shifter."

"The other girls held with me had minor magical talents from what I saw. Nothing that could even come close to challenging the mage that had us. At least, not after he'd already bled them. I was the biggest threat, so he kept me extra weak. Kept slicing me with his evil athame."

Her voice had grown bitter, but Ezra didn't blame her. All he could do was be here for her now and let her know she was safe. Or, at least, as safe as he could make her under the changed circumstances in this town.

"Athame?" King asked, sounding curious. "That's like a ritual knife or something, right?"

"Yes," she replied. "A ritual dagger is used by many witches in certain traditions, but they are never used to harm anyone. It's more a symbolic thing. Blood path mages use their athames to cause pain, make beings bleed and steal their power. Same word, totally different concept. What makes the difference is the intent of the wielder and the usage."

"You seem to know a lot about witchcraft for a shifter," King complimented her, but she shook her head.

"I learned the hard way, at the hands of a sociopath." Thea sighed heavily, as if to release the bad memories.

"What worries me," Ace put in after a moment of silence, "is that we don't have the kind of firepower Ezra had when he took down the bastard that had you, Thea. As far as I know, it's just us. We don't have any mages, and we don't have any backup. Unless you have a team of Wraiths hiding out in the hills, waiting for a call." Ace looked at Ezra hopefully, but Ez had to shake his head.

"While I wish I did have that kind of support lined up, though I'll make a few calls. On such short notice, I don't know if any of my contacts could get here in time. But, from what I understand, the mage that had Thea was an old-timer with special skills and a rare gift of clairvoyance that allowed him to stay one step ahead of all those who had pursued him for decades. He'd also had vast experience messing in the lives of humans and shifters alike. Whoever's operating here isn't quite up to the same caliber in that regard. The whole plan to make two wolf Packs fight just seems a bit clumsy to me. We might have caught a bit of a break," Ezra told them. "Still, it's not going to be easy, but we're bears. We can handle pretty much anything a single human mage can throw at us, right?"

That last bit was more bravado than certainty, but Ezra felt the need to rally the troops after Thea's revelations. She'd told her story with courage, and Ezra couldn't fault her. Not one bit. But they didn't need to focus on the negative aspects of the mission they'd set for themselves. No, this was the time for planning, and believing they could do what they set out to do was half the battle, in his experience.

CHAPTER SIX

The food order arrived, and conversation turned more general. Thea felt relieved. Remembering her own suffering at the hands of Bolivar—while an important part of her recovery—was also still difficult. Luckily, the brothers seemed to realize that, and they took the conversation in other directions.

She learned that, while the brothers looked almost like they could be triplets, there was actually more than a decade between each of them. Shifters lived longer than humans and stayed in their prime throughout most of their long lives. They talked about themselves and their family a bit, then the talk turned to the events in town as the restaurant began to fill up with people and discussion of anything shifter-related became more difficult.

After hearing the entertainment options available for the evening, it was decided that all five of them would go to a concert that night. The men had their own reasons for wanting to go, and the hints that they were able to give in the now-crowded restaurant led Thea to believe that they would be observing the crowd more than the show.

They spent a bit more than the standard hour eating lunch, but since the brothers were visiting experts and not regular employees of the garage, they were comfortable making their own hours—or so they told Thea when she inquired. It was mid-afternoon by the time Ezra and Thea went back to the hotel. He went to work, making the promised phone calls, while Thea retreated to her bedroom to place a call back home.

Her parents hadn't been too keen on her desire to roam, but she'd promised to keep in touch with them. She'd called every other day and knew it would probably reassure them to know that she wasn't traveling alone any longer. They'd met Ezra when they'd come to collect her from Lake Tahoe. They'd said many times how grateful they were that she'd been rescued by a fellow bear shifter and that his intervention had probably saved her life and her bear spirit.

Her dad was a strong bear, but neither of her parents really had an Alpha presence. At least not among other bears. It didn't matter, though. They lived quiet lives, on the outskirts of a small shifter community where they were the only bears in the immediate area. The nearest Alpha bear lived on the outskirts and wasn't seen very often in town. Of course, just by virtue of their animal spirit and the size of their shifted forms, both her mother and father were well respected by the Others.

As she'd expected, her folks were overjoyed that she'd met up with Ezra and was now *traveling with* him, as they put it. Her mother insisted that the hand of Fate had stepped in to put Thea in Ezra's path—or the other way around.

Either way, it totally worked for her mom. She'd liked Ezra from the beginning, and Thea knew without question that her mom would love to have a bear like Ezra for a son-in-law. She'd said so often enough since Thea had gone back home.

Thea wisely didn't mention any of the magical problems in town. As far as her folks were concerned, the bike rally was just a nice little diversion on her journey of self-discovery.

Her mom asked if Thea planned to stay with Ezra after the rally was over, but Thea told her mom, quite honestly, that she had no idea what she would do after.

Right now, Thea wasn't thinking any further than surviving the coming ordeal with an evil mage and two wolf Packs ready to kill each other. She hadn't expected to ever run into trouble like this again, but if she had to face her worst fears, she was glad Ezra was nearby. He'd saved her once, and though she didn't ever want to require saving again, she was glad he was around. He made her feel safer...and stronger.

Her experiences had changed her. She'd gained in strength and dominance. She was more Alpha than her folks now, and that had made things a little tricky at home as she'd grown healthier and more able to get around. She'd left as much for their good as her own.

She loved them, and she'd never pull dominance on them on purpose, but her bear was learning its way and wasn't quite sure of when to be fierce and when to back down. It didn't make any sense to take the chance that she would hurt her parents' feelings while experimenting with her new sense of self.

She spent a bit more time on the call than she'd planned, but it felt really good to talk to her folks. They'd been so supportive of her recovery.

She'd hated leaving them to go on this trip, but had known it was something she just had to do. Maybe there really was something to her mother's belief in the hand of Fate.

When she came out of her bedroom, Ezra was just ending his own call, and he was frowning. She didn't want to pry, but she also wanted him to know she was there for him if he needed help.

"Anything I can do?" she asked, heading for the kitchenette and the coffee he must've made while she'd been in her room.

"I called Gabe and Margo," Ezra told her. "They say hello,

by the way, and they were glad to hear you're doing so well." That made Thea feel good, but the immediate problem here in town took precedence over her personal stuff. "They're going to try to get here, but they may not be able to make it in time. Which means we're probably on our own with the mage."

"It's nice of them to try," Thea said, hoping the other couple would arrive before she and the other bears had to confront the magic being used against the werewolves in this town.

They talked about their plans for the evening, and Thea passed on greetings from her folks to Ezra, then she went back into her bedroom to get ready for the night ahead. She put on a different outfit and did her hair and makeup with care. Ezra was taking her out to dinner, then they would meet up with the bear brothers at the concert, which was being held on one of the streets in town that had been closed off to traffic especially for the rally.

Dinner was hearty, in a crowded restaurant filled with bikers from all over. Things were really in full swing now, and the little town was chock full of people. They kept the conversation light, and Thea took note of the admiring glances Ezra drew from some of the bolder human women. It made her feel a little aggressive and a bit proud at the same time.

He was with *her*. And any woman who made a play for him in any way was going to bleed. *Grr.*

Not that Ezra gave them any encouragement. He barely seemed to notice the female attention sent his way.

He didn't acknowledge any of the sultry glances and gave everyone a bland smile, if anything, when socially necessary. He was polite but not encouraging, which made her inner bear settle.

After dinner, they headed down the crowded street to the venue where a country rock band was already playing. It was the opening act, and they weren't bad at all. In fact, Thea found herself nodding slightly to the beat. The band had a good groove and an excellent singer.

Ezra spotted the brothers over by one of the many bar stalls that had been set up around the perimeter of the open-air venue. When they met up, Jack handed Thea a beer he'd bought for her, and King handed one to Ezra, receiving thanks in return, as well as an offer to get the next round.

They watched the opening act for a little while, standing on the edge of the crowd, back by the refreshments. Thea enjoyed the music, but she got the feeling the men were watching the people around them a lot more than the people on stage. She took a quick glance around and realized there were a few familiar faces she had seen at the garage that afternoon.

Many of the local werewolves had come to the concert. She sidled a little closer to Ezra and put her arm in his.

"Is the other side here, too?" she asked in a low voice.

"I think so," he told her. "See that guy in the white Stetson hat?"

He nodded toward a tall, rangy man ambling toward one of the bigger wolves they'd seen that morning at the shop. When they bumped into each other—clearly on purpose—she thought a fistfight was going to break out right then and there.

Thankfully, saner heads prevailed as they both looked around at the gathering of humans, then settled on growling at each other as they walked away. She thought she saw the one facing her mouth the word *tomorrow*, but she couldn't really be sure from her position, about twenty yards away, with people milling around in the middle.

"Those are the two leaders," Ace said quietly. He was standing next to her, with Ezra on her other side and Ace's two brothers watching their backs. She knew Ezra could hear his words, but seeing as how they were in a noisy crowd with so many humans around, they were being circumspect in what they said. "The guy in the white hat is from White Oaks out of Iowa. The other is a local guy. They call their territory the Southern Buttes."

"Looks like they're keeping it together until tomorrow," Ezra observed.

"Yeah, thankfully," Ace replied, sighing with a hint of relief. "It would be a real problem if they started losing their shit in the middle of all this."

And by *this*, she knew he meant all the humans around. The vast majority of the planet didn't know a thing about shifters, and they wanted it kept that way.

It was just safer for all concerned. But she thought she knew why the two werewolf Alphas were waiting to start their fight.

"It suits the bad guy's purpose. To do it here would confuse the issue for him and muddy the waters. He wouldn't get as clean a power boost," she told them, speaking quietly. "He'll want to do this in an isolated location where he can control things and reap the most reward out of the event."

She glanced at Ezra and Ace, on either side of her. Both had thoughtful expressions on their faces now.

"That makes a lot of sense, disgusting as it is to think of someone able to pull their strings to such an extent," Ace replied after a long moment of thought.

"We just need to know where. And exactly when," Ezra put in, a muscle in his jaw ticking with tension as he kept his eyes firmly on the crowd in front of them.

"I can probably tell you when," Thea put in. "Tomorrow night is a full moon. He'll probably pull the trigger as the moon starts to rise. As it travels towards its zenith is the most powerful time. When it's in decline back to the horizon, it's weakening. As it rises, it's strengthening."

Ezra looked at her, his brows drawn down in a frown. "How do you know?"

"I listened," she told him with a shrug that was much lighter than the memories that had just been dragged up. "Um... He would talk sometimes," she said, hoping Ezra would know which *he* she meant without her having to say the bastard's name out in the open where anyone might hear and recognize the name Bolivar. "I learned a bit about how and why he chose to do things at particular times."

Ace nodded. "Jack said something similar. He knows more about it than me and King."

"So, now, we just need to know where," Ezra said again.

"Someplace isolated where he can control access," Thea said. "Probably away from all the hubbub in town."

"We'll do some analysis of the terrain," Ace said. "What are you guys doing after the concert?" At that point, Thea knew they were all going to be spending some time poring over maps after the show was over.

"We've got a big table we can work on if you don't have room," Ezra told Ace. "And we can order in snacks."

"Sounds like a plan," Ace replied, and then, they settled in to watch the rest of the show.

There were no more incidents involving the werewolves from the garage that Thea could see, but the men were watching the crowd for the rest of the performance, and maybe they saw some things she didn't from their slightly higher vantage point. She'd always been tall for a woman, but her animal spirit was huge, and shifters were usually fit and healthy but a bit taller than their human counterparts. Still, standing next to these big men, Thea felt downright dainty.

She felt so safe in Ezra's presence. The other guys were great, too, and they added an extra layer of security, but it was Ezra that made her feel truly protected, in the very best possible way.

She realized more and more that she hadn't been dreaming when she'd been attracted to Ezra way back when they'd first met. Sure, he'd saved her life, but there was something more to the instinct that drew her to him than just gratitude for his brave actions.

She was even more attracted to him now, if that was even possible. Now that her bear was back at full strength—and then some—and her spirit was recovering along with her body, she was even more drawn to the big man at her side. He was good-looking, sure, but that wasn't all there was to him. He had depths she was only just starting to know, and she admired the man she was discovering beneath the handsome exterior.

What's more, she thought he just might be attracted to her, too. She had to stop and think about that for a moment, not really daring to hope that maybe, somehow, they could get together. Maybe for a fling. Or, maybe...for something a little more permanent.

She knew for sure her mother would be bouncing with happiness if it turned out that Ezra was Thea's mate. And there it was. The M word. Could he really be her mate?

She'd always imagined that she'd know immediately if she ever met her perfect match, but the way she'd met Ezra had been...confusing, at best. So much had happened to her that she doubted very much that she would have even recognized herself, had she been able to look in a mirror, when they first met.

She'd been a mess. Her animal spirit at its lowest ebb of energy before fading away entirely.

Ezra had brought her bear back to life. He'd held on to the tiny spark that her bear had been reduced to, and had protected that spirit, encouraging it to take power from his immense heart and to live.

Thea very much doubted her bear would have survived without him. And, without her bear...she wouldn't have survived, either.

He'd saved them both, giving her a chance to live on and thrive. She owed him a lot for his bravery and willingness to put himself on the line for others, but that wasn't the only reason she was attracted to him. It was Ezra himself. His inner character and the quiet strength he exuded at every turn.

He was solid. Intelligent. Steadfast. Like some kind of knight of old, he was a born protector, willing and able to fight for what was right, but level-headed about it. She admired him in so many ways.

And he was totally hot, too, of course. He was tall and broad shouldered. Lean and intensely focused. She liked that about him.

Actually…she liked everything about him. His new job sounded intriguing, and she liked the idea that he'd taken on the role of troubleshooter—or champion, in her eyes—for folks who were trying to clean up their little part of the world and rid it of crime and evil.

It was a noble thing he was doing. Maybe a little dangerous at times, too, but he was an Alpha bear. He could handle himself. She had confidence in his abilities and his judgment, which made it a little less scary all around.

At the end of the show, all five bear shifters headed back on foot to Ezra's hotel suite, which was only a few blocks away. Ezra called in an order to a local restaurant that delivered several bags of hot food about forty minutes later. By that time, they'd taken over the table at one end of the main room and laid out some maps Ezra seemed to have sourced from somewhere.

Thea had never really seen a topographical map in person before, but she thought that's what they were. There were also road maps with the highways and lanes laid out neatly and color coded.

Thea didn't really want to intrude on what seemed like a high-tech strategy session. The guys were talking in grid coordinates like they were some kind of Spec Ops team… And, maybe…they were. She didn't really know what any of them had done before she'd met them. She knew Ezra had been a bounty hunter and was now a corporate troubleshooter, but from the way he and the other guys were talking, she wouldn't be surprised to learn they'd all spent time in the military.

She tried to follow some of the jargon but got lost pretty fast. It didn't matter, though. She was tired, and they were well occupied by their discussion of terrain, high ground, line of sight and other things she couldn't really decipher.

She decamped to her bedroom and got ready for bed, happy to leave the guys to their planning. She'd shared everything she could for one day. Now, it was their turn to do what they knew best.

CHAPTER SEVEN

Thea wasn't sure what woke her a few hours later, but she got up somewhere around three a.m. and made a quick trip to the bathroom, then went out into the kitchen area to get some ice water. That always hit the spot when she woke up in the middle of the night. She'd had a lot of nightmares after her rescue and was familiar with the wee hours of the morning, sadly.

What she wasn't used to was Ezra coming out to see if she was okay. He opened his bedroom door, and she spun around to look at him in surprise. She gasped. His chest was bare, and he wore only loose pajama bottoms, his bare feet peeping out from the baggy pool of fabric as he walked toward her.

"You okay?" he asked in a growly tone that made her insides quiver. "I heard you get up."

"Sorry I disturbed you. I'm fine. Just wanted some water." She turned resolutely back to the sink to complete her task. She would not ogle his magnificent chest. She would *not*.

"You seem tense," he murmured, coming up behind her. He put his big hands on her shoulders and began rubbing in slow circles. She felt like melting into a little puddle on the floor. "Bad dream?" he asked in that same low, sexy voice.

She shook her head, unable to come up with actual words. Not when he was touching her like that.

The slow circles turned into a true massage as he worked the tension she didn't know she had out of her shoulder muscles. She groaned as the stress released. She'd been in knots and hadn't really realized it until they were gone.

As the tension drained away, a new lethargy crept into her body, along with an awareness of how close he was standing, how good his hands felt on her, how delicious his scent was in her nose. Everything just felt...right.

When he leaned fractionally closer and rubbed his nose along the back of her neck, she shivered with delight. Yes, that's what she wanted. Him. Closer.

When his lips trailed along the skin beneath her ear, she squirmed.

"You smell delicious," he told her as she tilted her head to give him greater access.

"So do you," she whispered, unable to say anything more creative. "You always have."

And he really had. He'd always scented of something right in her world. Something she could cling to and something that would give her strength as she gave in return.

Dear sweet Mother of All. Was he her mate?

The thought gave her pause. What if he was?

Aside from her mother's expected joy at the news, what would it mean to Thea personally? Ezra was all that was good and true in the world, and she respected him greatly, but did she love him? Did she love him the way she'd always dreamed she'd love her mate?

Although the waters had been muddied by her capture and recovery, she realized suddenly that she probably did. She'd loved him for a long time, but with everything that had happened, she hadn't really understood it until this moment.

She sent a prayer of thanks skyward and turned in his arms, searching for his gaze in the darkened room. It didn't matter. They were bear shifters. They could see well in the dark, even in human form.

What she saw in his gaze gave her pause. He looked...worried?

"I'm sorry, Thea. I got a little carried away." He tried to move away, but she grabbed his forearms, stopping his motion.

"Do you want me, Ezra?" she asked, feeling bold in the dark of the night.

She saw the truth on his face before he spoke the word. "Yes."

"How long?" she pressed. "How long have you wanted me?"

"A long time," he admitted. She read nothing but honesty in his gaze. "At first, I wanted to protect you and care for you. My bear wanted to drag you home to my den and keep you safe for always, but it was more than just the protective instinct. My bear recognized it well before my human half, though that wasn't too far behind. You're just...mine, Thea. You're my mate." He looked so serious as his words thrilled through her heart. "I knew it almost right away, but I also knew you'd been badly hurt and you needed time to heal. I was willing to give you time. As much time as you needed. But I would have found you at some point, and if you were able to return my feelings, I knew I would ask you to be my mate, for now and for always."

"And if I didn't return those feelings?" she asked, needing to know how deeply he felt, though her heart thrilled each time he called her his mate.

"Then, I would have let you go and lived out the rest of my days alone. You're the only woman for me, Thea. I knew that from almost the first moment I scented you. Even as hurt as you were, I knew you were meant for me."

"What would you say if I told you that I felt the same?" Now that she had come to the critical moment, she felt a little giddy with hope for their future.

His eyes lit up, the magic of his bear half shining through

his chocolate brown eyes. "You do?"

"I do," she affirmed, nodding with no hesitation. "You're my mate, too."

Ezra leaned close and kissed her, taking her lips with authority, and a gentleness that stole her breath. He was warm and hard in all the right places, his body muscular against her softness as he drew her closer.

Her bear spirit rose up in triumph as she connected with her mate for the very first time in passion. It was about time. That was the overwhelming sense from her animal side. Her human side gasped as Ezra's hands roamed over her body, touching her in all the right places and making her yearn for more. So much more...

Ezra broke the kiss, and before she could even protest, he bent down and scooped her into his arms. His strength was on tantalizing display as he carried her into his bedroom as if she weighed no more than a feather. He placed her on the bed, handling her like she was made of spun glass, and then, he just stood back a little and looked at her.

Their eyes met, the power of his bear swirling in his gaze as her own bear's magic was probably showing in her own eyes. Man to woman. Bear to bear. Alpha to Alpha.

That's what was so special about this. They were meeting as equals.

That was something that had never happened to her before. She'd changed as a result of the turmoil that had led her to this moment. She was Alpha now. She no longer fit comfortably into her family group, but with Ezra...she fit. He respected what she was now and wasn't overpowered by it. Far from it.

He was just as strong—if not stronger—than she was. She couldn't intimidate him, and he couldn't dominate her. It was a perfect match, in that way, and she hoped to find out soon all the other ways they matched.

That thought in mind, she reached up and took his hand, pulling him downward, demanding gently that he join her on the bed. She was wearing only a silky nightgown she'd had in her saddlebags. He wore only those silly pajama pants.

Those had to go. She pushed at his waistband as he came down next to her, and succeeded in sliding those baggy pajamas down his hips, exposing the fact that he wasn't wearing anything beneath them. *Yes.* She finally had an answer to the naughty questions that had been circling in her mind. He *was* just as well built as she'd suspected.

Sculpted by the hand of a loving Goddess, his body was the stuff of female fantasies. Rippling abs pointed to a hard cock that she could imagine would bring her the greatest pleasure. Reaching out, she took him in her hand, loving the growl that came from deep in his chest when she touched him intimately.

"Keep that up, and this isn't going to last very long," he warned her playfully.

"That's okay," she told him. "We have the rest of the night all to ourselves."

"Mm. I like the sound of that."

Ezra slid his hand under her nightie, lifting the silky fabric higher and higher, tantalizing her with his slow, deliberate motions. She still had hold of him, but she lost her ability to focus on anything but the way his hand was circling around her thigh and heading for the spot that so wanted his touch. She moved her legs apart, inviting him to check out what was hidden between, but he wouldn't be rushed. Ezra took his time and drove her passions higher with every teasing touch until finally—finally—his fingers found the soft folds that ached to be explored.

She moaned as his hand slipped more fully between her thighs. His gaze met hers, and it was all she could do to remember to breathe.

"How do you want this, honey? Fast or slow?" he asked, all the while, sliding his finger around near her clit.

She hadn't worn panties to bed, and now, she was very thankful for that small mercy. Had she somehow hoped they'd end up in bed together when she dressed for bed earlier that night? Yeah, she probably had. If not consciously, then her subconscious had been guiding her, the little hussy.

"Fast," she gasped as he hit her button and made her whole body clench as delicious sensations washed over her.

"You sure?" He was teasing now, rubbing her clit with little back and forth motions that stole her breath. All she could do was nod her agreement as he grinned like a fool. A talented, handsome, sexually gifted fool. *Her* fool.

She had let go of his hard cock somewhere along the way, and he was free to move about, splaying her out on the bed while he ran his hands over her silky nightgown, raising it up and then over her shoulders, but leaving it on her arms. He deliberately tangled her hands in the fabric. It wasn't any real barrier to her movement. She could have easily ripped through the silk with her bear strength. But just the idea of it acting as a restraint was kind of hot.

She smiled up at him as he placed his big hands over her breasts, learning their curve and feel. He played with her nipples before bending to take each one in his mouth, licking and sucking in a way that made her squirm. Her hands were up above her head, and there was a feeling of imagined vulnerability that really *worked* with Ezra, where it probably wouldn't have worked with any other man.

She could allow herself to feel vulnerable with him because she knew in her heart of hearts that he would never hurt or betray her. She'd already trusted him with her life. Trusting him with her body was a no-brainer.

She was happy to let this encounter develop in any direction he wanted it to go. There would be time for her to lead their love making later. This first time, she wanted to be the damsel to his dashing Alpha presence. Her inner bear wanted it, too, which meant it was definitely the right course of action for this moment out of time.

She loved looking at him as he prowled above her. She'd never been much for the missionary position, but then again, she'd never really had sex with a man who matched her so well, body and spirit. All of her previous experience—what little there was of it—had been with humans who hadn't had a clue about her bear half. They'd thought her adventurous and a little wild, but none of the men she'd dated seriously had ever stirred her bear to anything other than mere tolerance.

It was kind of sad, actually. She'd thought she might go through life drifting from one man to another, never finding the one who could stir her animal side into the kind of devotion she saw in her parents' relationship. They were true mates. She wanted that for herself.

And now, she had it. She had *him*. Ezra. Hunky bear of a man who both challenged and coddled her. So far, he'd been a genius at knowing which to do at just the right time.

He was also proving to be a genius at bringing out the most of her sexual responses. The light trailing of his fingers over her skin did more to rouse her passions that the most intimate touches from any of her other lovers. They were total amateurs when compared to Ezra. He played her body like a master conducting a symphony of his own creation.

She moaned and writhed under his skilled fingers, until finally, he came down over her, positioning his muscular legs between hers, the head of his cock just grazing the place she wanted him to enter so badly. He paused, looking deep into her eyes.

"Do you want me, Thea?"

What was he, kidding? He'd have to be both blind and deaf to doubt her need for him at this moment. But maybe he needed verbal confirmation. Maybe he was wary of pushing her into something she didn't fully understand? That was kind of sweet. Even if it meant he was keeping her waiting.

"I do," she assured him. "I've wanted you for a long time. I've dreamed of this, Ezra. Now, will you *please* just give me what I want?"

He chuckled as he shook his head. "Well, that couldn't be any clearer," he muttered, smiling. "Hold on to my shoulders now," he coached her as he began a slow slide within that didn't end until he was completely sheathed in her welcoming warmth.

Dear, sweet Goddess! That felt good.

"All right?" he asked, his breathing a bit unsteady as he seemed to be trying to hold himself back.

She nodded, unable to really speak at the moment. Things were just a wee bit overwhelming in the best possible way. Then, he began to move, and she lost her mind entirely.

He stroked deep, pushing her higher with each motion. Her body trembled and then bucked and shivered beneath him as climax after climax took her over. He rode her through each, taking her higher on the next until she nearly blacked out.

Thea had heard about multiple orgasms, but she had figured they were like unicorns—the stuff of legend. Not so, she was surprised and very pleased to learn. Perhaps she'd been waiting for this moment for so very long, her body was primed and ready. She was overdue for a release the likes of which she had never experienced.

She came with a moan of delight as Ezra finally stiffened above her, emptying himself, body and soul, into her waiting arms as they joined together in the most intensely passionate experience of her life. The bliss lasted long moments, shooting her higher, pushing her body farther, lengthening the pleasure until she wasn't sure where she began and he ended. The only thing that mattered was that they were together.

As it should be.

They dozed and then woke to make love once more. This time, Thea took the lead, showing him what she liked from the top and learning what he liked her to do for him. It was a lesson she would spend the rest of her life happily repeating.

They slept again afterward, Thea snuggled deep into Ezra's arms. She'd never slept better in her life than she did with him next to her.

CHAPTER EIGHT

The next morning, Thea was gone from the bed when Ezra woke. The spot next to him was still warm from her body heat, so she couldn't have been gone long. He heard the water start up in the shower, and the mystery was solved. He wondered for a moment if he should join her, but then, he looked at the clock and realized they'd slept in. He had work to do today if he was going to avert a werewolf disaster tonight.

The relationship was new, too. He didn't want to presume things or push her too far, too fast. It was enough that they had admitted their feelings for each other last night. In time, he'd get to learn what she was comfortable with from him and vice versa. For now, he'd give her a little bit of space. Not much. His bear wouldn't allow him to let her roam free or too far away from him. But he could give her a solo shower, though he sorely wanted to share it with her.

Ezra rolled out of bed and headed for the kitchenette to get the coffee going. If he wasn't going to waylay her in the sudsy water, the least he could do was provide breakfast for his mate.

Mate. *Mmm*. He liked the way that sounded.

He'd almost given up on ever finding that one woman who could share the rest of his days. And then, he'd found her. Thea. Bloody and nearly broken, locked inside a cage in a dingy basement. His heart had known her the moment he'd seen her, but he had also known that she would need time—probably a lot of it—before she was ready to be with him. He'd despaired of her ever being ready, but Fate had been kind and thrown them together again.

This time, they were both ready for the consequences of recognizing and claiming their mate. They might have a few battles to fight as they rolled along in life, but from now on, they'd do it together. He loved that idea.

Ezra's phone rang as he was pulling out the ingredients from the small refrigerator to make breakfast. He answered, still setting things up even as he took the call.

"Jack and Ace are down at the shop," King told Ezra as soon as they'd exchanged greetings. "I'm on a parts run, so Ace asked me to check in with you. Jack's about losing his mind. He hasn't been able to tell us much, but judging by the expression on his face, there's a heavy load of magic going down at the shop today. He doesn't look happy."

"Tell him to get out of there if it gets to be too much. Are you sure you and Ace aren't affected by whatever it is that's got the wolves?" Ezra asked bluntly.

"Nah, it just slides right off my fur, whatever it is. I mean, I feel something in the air, but it's like a cloud of gnats and just as easily ignored. Ace said the same. Jack feels it more than we do, but he's always been more sensitive than either of us," King replied. "But his sensitivity also makes him more resistant, so I wouldn't worry about us three. It's the wolves that are about to go ape shit."

Ezra had stopped moving as King gave his report. Thea came out of her bedroom, dressed in tight jeans and a stretchy top that made him want to tug it off and lick her all over. Ezra cleared his throat and tried to get his mind off his luscious mate and back on business.

"I plan to do some scouting of the two wolf Packs today," he said, stalling for time as Thea sashayed over. She placed her hands on his shoulder and arm then stretched up to kiss his cheek.

"You'll probably find the local Alpha, and a good portion of the Pack that isn't at the garage, down at the pool hall over on the north side of town. Top dog's name is Chase Rivers. This time of year, he's pretty much there all day. He and his Pack bought the joint a few years back, and they cater to the tourists for the income, though usually they don't mix much with outsiders."

During King's revelations, Thea had relieved Ezra of the frying pan that he'd been holding and sauntered to the stove to pick up breakfast prep. Just like that.

One part of Ezra's brain spun with the changes in his life. He had a mate now. Someone to pick up the slack when he got distracted by things like business phone calls. He'd wanted to make breakfast to show Thea that he cared and would provide for her. The sharing of food was important to his bear side. But Thea was doing the cooking now, and she was showing him the same, in reverse.

The thought of it hit him right in his heart, where a little piece melted and winged its way over to her. He realized that love was a two-way street. He loved her and wanted to take care of her, but she wanted to care for him in return.

It had been a very long time since anyone had wanted to take care of Ezra. It had been a very long time since he'd wanted anyone to do so. But, with Thea, everything was new and shiny. Special and intense.

The part of his mind that wasn't blown by her casual actions tried really hard to regroup and concentrate on what King was telling him. Luckily, the other man didn't seem to notice Ezra's inattention.

"The visiting Pack is on the east end of town. They take over a good portion of a small motel with a roadhouse next door down by the highway. They hail from Iowa, and their Alpha is named Brock Hanson. Word is, he's always been a reasonable sort of fellow, and the two Packs enjoyed a good relationship in years past, but this year, everything's different. Nobody can tell me exactly what the Iowa Pack did to piss the locals off, but they all claim whatever it was is unforgivable and requires a blood price be paid. Preferably by every single member of that Pack. The locals are definitely on the warpath, and it's going to take some fancy footwork to stop this before it becomes pitched battle."

Able to focus a little better by deliberately *not* watching Thea's butt wiggling as she stood in front of the small stove, Ezra sat down at the table with his back to the kitchenette. He thought through what King had told him.

"All right. This is what we'll do. Thea and I will swing by the local Pack's place this morning and introduce ourselves to the Alpha. See if he can be reasoned with and check him out for ourselves. Then, we'll head to that roadhouse you mentioned next to the visiting Pack's motel and see if we can't do the same with them. It's time for some serious recon," Ezra said, knowing Thea could hear his side of the conversation and would know he wasn't shutting her out of his plans. They were a team now, and he had to give her the choice of whether or not she wanted to be part of this op or not.

He'd prefer she stay on the sidelines, somewhere safe, but he also sensed she probably needed this. She needed to confront her worst fear and rise above it. This was a good opportunity—with him at her side and the three powerful brothers as backup, plus whoever else could make it here in time, as the cavalry—to face down evil and some of her past issues in as safe a manner as possible.

Not that there wouldn't be danger. There would. Plenty of it. But they were bears. They were tough. Rugged. And Thea had to get a feel for her new strength under battlefield conditions. She had to learn how far she could trust herself and her new mate. He wanted her to be strong and to know herself as well as she possibly could. Only then could she heal from her past horrors completely.

"After lunch, we'll probably head over to the garage and confer with your guys," Ezra went on as Thea came over to the table and started putting out dishes.

"Sounds good," King replied, going on to iron out a few more details.

Meanwhile, Thea finished cooking breakfast and began serving it up. Ezra smiled his thanks at her even as he finished talking with King and ended the call a few minutes later.

"Sorry about that. I meant to make you breakfast," he told her, taking her hand as she sat down at the place next to him.

"No problem," she replied with a shy sort of smile that made him think about the night they'd spent in each other's arms. "I'm not the world's greatest cook, but I think I make okay omelets." She gestured toward his plate as he let go of her hand and picked up the fork she'd laid out for him.

"This looks great." He began eating and then was sure to compliment her on each facet of the meal. The fact was, she'd gone out of her way to make breakfast for them both, and he was touched more than he could say by the simple gesture.

After breakfast, Ezra took a quick shower, and then, the two of them headed across town for their first recon stop of the day. The pool hall wasn't busy at this time of the morning, which was perfect, as far as Ezra was concerned. He'd come here to meet the local wolf Alpha face to face— something that was best done without a bunch of humans around.

When he walked into the pool hall with Thea at his side, he immediately felt the scrutiny of more than a dozen sets of wolf shifter eyes. The Alpha was seated at the bar along one wall, sipping coffee while perusing some kind of ledger book spread out on the bar top in front of him. He turned to look at them as they approached.

"Well, will you look what the cat dragged in," the man said, standing from the bar stool.

He was as tall as Ezra, though not nearly as wide. The

werewolf's frame was rangy and lean, muscular but lithe in a way Ezra's bear bulk couldn't match. Ezra didn't mind in the least. He liked being able to pound just about anyone or anything into the ground.

"I hear you're the top dog in this town," Ezra said, knowing some of the Pack would take offense at the words but wanting to gauge their reactions for himself.

He wasn't afraid of any piddling little werewolf. Even a dozen of them wasn't cause for concern. It's only when the Packs went hunting as a whole that any bears in the vicinity might sit up and take notice.

The Alpha of the Southern Buttes Pack just stood his ground, looking Ezra up and down as if considering whether or not he could take him. Good.

So far, the local Alpha didn't seem like a total hothead, even if his eyes were a bit glassier than Ezra would've liked to see them. A quick glance at the werewolves in various positions around the big room told him they all held the glassy eyes of the bespelled. Not good.

"What brings you here, Teddy?" the Alpha wolf asked, being just as disrespectful as Ezra had been. Well, the boy had some balls to stand up to a grizzly bear—that was a good sign in one way.

"Name's Ezra Tate. I'm a bounty hunter. It's my habit to check in with the local Alpha whenever I hit a new town. Just in case they take exception to my profession," Ezra said in a reasonable tone of voice.

"You on the hunt here?" the Alpha challenged, his strong chin jutting upward.

"No," Ezra replied. "Just on vacation with my lady. We're newly mated. This is Thea." Ezra turned to Thea and smiled at her, winking as he introduced her so that she smiled, as well. Who could resist beautiful Thea's smile?

"Congratulations," the Alpha wolf said with genuine warmth in his tone. "May the blessings of the Goddess be upon your union," he added, a strange, somewhat confused look coming into his eyes as he said the ritualistic words. As if mention of the Mother of All was somehow trying to dull the evil magic that had been perpetrated on the Alpha wolf.

But it wasn't enough. Ezra could see the glazed look return almost immediately. They were going to need something big to break the mage's hold on these poor wolves. But what?

"I'm Chase Rivers, Alpha of the Southern Buttes Pack. You're welcome in town as long as you don't cause trouble for me and my Pack," the Alpha added, reaching out for a handshake with each of them in turn.

"We don't intend to cause any trouble. Just looking to have a good time," Ezra reassured the man. "Thing is, I heard some whispers that you were in conflict with another Pack of your kind, and there's a scent of unwelcome magic all over this town. I wanted to ask you, Alpha to Alpha, what was happening and if there's any way conflict could be averted—or at least delayed until all the visiting humans leave town."

Chase's gaze hardened. "White Oaks needs to bleed. We won't do it in sight of the humans, but it's going to happen. There's nothing that can stop it now."

They spent a good twenty minutes talking with the Alpha, trying to learn what the problem was, but he wasn't very clear on it at all. He just kept repeating the need to kill as many White Oaks wolves as he could and that nothing was going to prevent it.

Otherwise coherent and seemingly normal, Chase was like a robot when it came to the subject of the other Pack, giving rote answers to any question Ezra or Thea posed. All answers leading to the end point that White Oaks had to die.

Eventually, Ezra gave up. He'd learned everything he was going to learn here. Even Thea's gentler interrogation methods had failed to elicit anything other than the canned response. They were beating a dead horse here, and he knew it.

Ezra extricated them from the pool hall as politely as possible, leaving on good terms with the local Pack and its Alpha. They headed back to where they'd parked their bikes in silence. Only when Thea was straddling her hog did she say anything.

"That was truly bizarre," she muttered.

Ezra turned to her and swept in for a quick kiss. "Those people are in trouble, for sure," he whispered in agreement, unsure if any of the people on the street were werewolves with superior hearing.

"I hope we can figure out a way to help them," she whispered back. Then, he kissed her again. His Thea with the soft heart. How he loved her.

CHAPTER NINE

When Thea entered the roadhouse out by the highway, she scented right away that the whole place was full of shifters. Wolves. Glassy-eyed wolves. Damn.

Nevertheless, she allowed Ezra to escort her to a table, where they were waited on by a shifter waitress. She was some kind of bird, if Thea's nose was accurate. The woman took their orders then casually added that everyone present was a shifter, so they could talk freely unless some humans showed up for lunch.

"Interesting," was Ezra's only comment. He took a rather obvious look around for himself and seemed to evaluate what he saw. "Mostly wolves," he stated to Thea

They both knew that the others could hear every word, if they wished to eavesdrop. Judging by the low conversations and lack of smiles on anyone's faces, Thea figured most of them *were* listening. This was not a happy crowd. Not by any stretch of the imagination.

Ezra kept talk general, mentioning the concert they'd seen the night before and then the modifications he was supposedly going to have made to his bike. Thea knew the phantom modifications were just a ruse they were using for him to keep returning to the bike shop to talk with the bear brothers. She told him a few harmless anecdotes about her family's reaction to her buying her bike, and the lunch passed in a pleasant enough way, even if they were being watched by almost every set of eyes in the place.

Eventually, when they were enjoying coffee after their meal, the waitress returned to their table with the check and a message. "The White Oaks Alpha would like to talk to you before you go. He's over there in the corner booth."

Ezra thanked the woman and gave her a wad of cash to cover both the meal and a generous tip. He then stood and politely assisted Thea before speaking.

"Do you want to go pay our respects?" he asked. She knew he was setting a scene, appearing reluctant when talking to the visiting Alpha was exactly why they had come here. This couldn't have worked out better had they planned it.

"Sure. I like wolves," she told him with a gamine grin.

They both knew she liked one wolf in particular—the woman who had helped save Thea and those other women from Bolivar, Margo Mahigan of the Stony Ridge Pack out of Canada. She'd made a real impression on Thea, and she admired the woman greatly.

They walked together over to the corner booth where the wolf Alpha sat with two others who looked like high-ranking Pack members. They were arranged one on either side of the Alpha, like some sort of honor guard.

Ezra walked right up to the table and said hello. The wolves saw him coming and stopped their own conversation to look him over. The two subordinates remained quiet while the Alpha wolf took a good long look at the bears in front of him.

"Forgive me for not standing, but I'm sort of stuck in the booth," the man said, with a friendly grin. "Pull up a chair and sit a spell. I don't often cross paths with bears, and I'd be interested in your take on the town and this strange situation we find ourselves in."

That little speech piqued Thea's interest, and she turned to Ezra and shrugged. He stole two chairs from a nearby empty table and put them on the open side of the booth. He waited for Thea to sit in a show of gentlemanly concern, then he sat beside her, leaning back casually.

"I'm Ezra Tate, and this is Thea, my mate," Ezra introduced them.

Thea felt a little thrill every time he said that. It was still so new and so...freaking perfect. She wondered if she'd ever get to the point where she took this amazing relationship for granted.

Nah. Not in this lifetime.

"Brock Hanson," the wolf Alpha replied. "My brother, Jim, and our Uncle Arch." Brock gestured to his left and his right.

The brother was obviously younger, but the uncle was still a wolf in his prime. He had a tough glint in his eye as he looked Ezra over, and she felt a little shiver. That uncle wasn't anyone to mess around with.

"So, what's this situation you were talking about?" Ezra asked casually.

If Thea hadn't known they'd come here specifically for a chance at this conversation, she wouldn't have realized it was anything special from Ezra's cool reaction. She was impressed with his composure.

"I noticed you and your posse watching the crowd at the concert last night. You saw what happened with the local wolf Alpha," Brock said plainly, calling Ezra's bluff.

"We saw something," Ezra agreed quietly when Brock paused for reaction. "Looked like a whole mess of trouble brewing between two wolf Packs."

"That it is," Brock confirmed. Thea noticed that his eyes weren't quite as glassy as some of the others. Certainly not as bad as the local Alpha's had been. "We come here every year for the party. Usually, we have a cordial relationship with the local Pack and any other visitors that might show up. We all have this agreement that rally week is a time of truce. We don't want to cause trouble with so many humans around. It would be too easy to make a mistake we could never reverse, if you know what I mean."

Thea knew exactly what he was getting at. Every shifter lived in fear these days of being caught on some human's camera phone doing something that would out the existence of shifters.

It had been easier to avoid being seen in the old days, but in recent years, every phone had a hi-res camera in it that took digital images that could be sent around the world with the flick of a finger. There was no film to be confiscated and destroyed if someone really messed up and was seen.

All shifters lived in fear that someone was going to royally screw up and get the humans on the hunt for anyone that might be a little different. It was well within the realm of possibility.

Humans were easily spooked, and there were a lot of them. A lot more of them than there were shifters. If the humans went on the warpath, shifters wouldn't really stand a chance.

"This year, we came into town, as usual, and immediately, some kind of shitstorm started blowing from the local Pack. Their Alpha started ranting about something we're supposed to have done wrong, making weird allegations against some of our younger members. Pups, really. Youngsters that are under my protection." The Alpha looked around the room at those of his Pack that were in the building, and Thea could see there were quite a few younger members who were probably just teenagers on their first away-from-home trip. "I can't let them go after my Pack. Especially not the pups. That's just bullshit."

Brock's eyes took on a dazed look, and anger started to boil within. Thea was shocked by the way the magic sort of took over the formerly somewhat cool-headed man. Was the spell triggered by anger? Or did it cause it?

Thea tried to step in and diffuse some of the anger. Maybe a feminine voice would help?

"We heard something about a fight planned for tonight," she said quietly. "Is there anything we can do to help prevent it?"

All three wolves looked at her sharply. The Alpha and his little brother's eyes were glazed over with that glassy sheen she was becoming familiar with all over again. The uncle, though... He seemed a little less affected than the others.

"I don't see how anything can prevent the confrontation now," Arch said quietly, letting his relatives seethe quietly. Neither looked able to speak at the moment as their anger spiked higher than the conversation would normally have called for.

"Have you given any thought to the idea that this conflict might have been caused or influenced by outside forces?" she asked as gently as she could. Now, the Alpha and his brother were growling a bit under their breath.

Thea wasn't worried. She could handle a wolf or two—even an Alpha. Especially with Ezra at her side.

But their show of anger was very concerning. These wolves weren't rational. Except maybe for the uncle...a little bit.

"What kind of outside forces?" Uncle Arch asked quietly, still the only one of the three who remained at all able to converse somewhat normally, though his eyes weren't free from the glassy taint.

"A blood path mage," Ezra said, his words filled with authority.

Everyone in the room stilled. It got so quiet you could hear a pin drop. Arch spoke for his nephew, the Alpha, once more.

"Where did you get this intel?" He spoke directly to Ezra, soldier to soldier, it seemed.

"Take a look around you, man. Does any of this seem normal to you?" Ezra asked in return.

Arch shook his head, like a dog trying to shake off the damp. He seemed to be fighting the compulsion, or whatever it was, that had been set upon him. Good. Maybe he could overcome the spell.

"It's not enough," Arch ground out between tightly clenched teeth. "I feel something…strange…happening, but we need more proof," he said.

"More proof?" Thea couldn't keep silent any longer. "I've been where you are now. Trapped under the weight of a spell you don't understand, but that makes you act out of character. It makes you do whatever the mage wants you to. Like puppets on his string." Thea hated remembering what had happened in Bolivar's basement, but these wolves needed to realize they weren't alone. "I've been there, Arch. I know how difficult it is to fight it off, but if you don't, you could lose a lot of your Pack. A lot of your family." She looked deliberately at the youngest wolf at the table, Jim, and then back. "Admit it. You know something's really wrong here. You're being manipulated into a fight where many of you will bleed for someone else's pleasure. You have to feel that, don't you?" She paused to take a breath, hoping against hope that she was getting through to him. "You already have your proof."

The rest of the wolf Pack remained silent and still, as if in a trance. It was creepy.

The bird-shifter waitress and the rest of the staff of the road house just looked really, really nervous. They weren't as affected by the spell, but they also weren't in a position to do anything about it.

Thea took a good look at them and noted the similarities. They were all some kind of bird shifter. Probably all of one family.

"I can just…" Arch seemed to be fighting for every word, the only one of the Pack not completely under the spell, though the Alpha's eyes were not quite as glassy, and he watched in silence, at least part of his focus on the conversation at the table. "I hear what you're saying," Arch finally said. "It makes sense, but I can't see how to stop this snowball of shit heading straight for us."

"Maybe we can help," Ezra offered. "I've faced this kind

of thing before."

"Are you part of the group from Grizzly Cove?" Arch asked, his gaze narrowing on Ezra.

"Affiliated with, not part of. Not yet, at least, though we may consider that when it comes time for us to settle down." Ezra glanced at Thea. This was the first she'd heard of that plan, but it appealed to her.

She was willing to at least go take a look at the town she'd heard so much about. She'd wanted to see it, anyway. Whether or not she would want to live there remained to be seen.

"But you served." It was a statement that held a bit of a question, as well.

Ezra nodded. "Green Beret. You?"

"SEAL," Arch said quietly.

"Wait a minute. You're Archibald Hanson? No fucking way." Ezra's voice was filled with recognition and a hint of friendly awe.

"Guilty as charged." Arch bowed his head slightly in acknowledgement.

"Thea, this guy wrote the book on guerilla actions. He's a legend in the Spec Ops community."

Thea thought she understood what Ezra was saying, but it was clear Ezra was far more impressed by the uncle than the purported Alpha of the wolf Pack.

And now, she knew Ezra had been a Green Beret. A lot of things started to make sense, given that little tidbit of information.

She suspected there would be a learning curve as she really got to know her new mate. She hoped she had a bit of mystery left to reveal to him, as well, though she didn't have some secret Special Forces background to reveal. Still, there was her doll collection. She'd bet he wouldn't be prepared for *that* when they moved in together.

Thea stifled the smile that wanted to come out at that thought. This was a serious situation. She couldn't help it that, every time she thought about her future with Ezra in her life, she wanted to grin like a fool.

"I'll admit, I don't know exactly what that means, but if you're as tough as Ezra made that sound, then you need to help your nephew and your Pack," Thea told the older man respectfully. "You're all being messed with on a magical level. Look at the eyes of the werewolves in this town, and you might notice a glassy stare." Thea shivered as she glanced at the people wolves in the room around them. They were all staring into space, their eyes not right. Not right at *all*. "You're stronger than the spell, Arch," she encouraged the man.

"Why isn't it…affecting you?" It seemed to be more difficult for Arch to speak, and Thea worried that, somehow, the spell was getting stronger. All the wolves were spaced out. Was the mage doing something to them *right now*?

"We're bears," Thea shrugged. "The bird shifters who run this place don't seem to be affected that much either. Could be this mage is just targeting your two wolf Packs." That had to be it.

"Will you help us? I don't know…if I can hold out against this," Arch said, each word seeming to be harder for him to say.

Ezra sat up straight and looked at the other man with concern. "We'll do everything in our power to stop this before it starts, but if it comes down to a fight, try not to bleed the other wolves. If you remember anything, remember to help us stop the mage."

Arch nodded once and then seemed to give in and let the glassiness take his eyes. He, like the rest of the wolves in the road house, were sitting there like zombies. Waiting.

For what? Thea could only guess that there was some kind of signal that would come later that day to set them all off. Like a ticking time bomb. The calm before the storm.

"He's gone," Ezra said, standing. His face showed both concern and disgust. "Come on. We'd better see how the others are coping. It wouldn't be good for humans to see this." Ezra paused by the bar and the little cluster of bird shifters standing behind it, looking really agitated. "I'd close the place for the rest of the day. Or, at least until these wolves come out from under whatever has got them in its grip. Keep your kin inside if you can. There's evil afoot in this town, and it's coming for the wolves."

The eldest male of the bird shifters nodded and followed Ezra and Thea to the door. He and Ezra exchanged a few low words while Thea tried to hide her shock at the state the wolves were in. This was really terrible.

It was just like what had happened to the women she'd been held prisoner with in Lake Tahoe. This was bad. Bad, bad, bad.

The bird shifter elder locked the door behind Ezra and Thea, and they headed for their bikes. She knew they had been planning to go to the garage next, and that the local werewolves were probably split between their pool hall and the garage at this time of day. Hopefully, they were all contained and could be hidden from human sight until they were released from the spell, compulsion, or whatever it was.

Ezra was on the phone, and she heard him talking to Ace as they settled on their bikes. She could hear that Ace had sent Jack over to the pool hall as soon as the wolves they worked with had succumbed to the zombie-like state. Jack had secured the pool hall, locking the place up with the wolves inside and putting signs out saying the place would be closed for the rest of the day. King was doing the same for the garage, which was a little trickier, since there were humans coming in for scheduled appointments.

Ace and his brothers would try to handle the humans and pack them off as quickly as possible, but She heard Ezra volunteer them to help. A moment later, the phone call was over, and she and Ezra were heading for the garage as quickly as possible.

They spent the rest of the afternoon running interference. Thea kept the wolves in the back room, coaxing them into seated positions and watching over them as they completely zoned out. Ezra and the other bears did what they could to fill in the gaps and handle as many of the human customers as possible.

Thea also made calls, using the appointment book and doing what she could to lighten the load by rescheduling folks to tomorrow or the next day wherever possible. They weren't happy about it, but they complied with her requests to change dates and times for the most part. She figured this would all be over by tomorrow, and they'd deal with the fallout, then. For now, the fewer humans coming to the repair shop, the better.

Around closing time, the wolves started to wake up. It was a slow process, and none of them seemed to realize they'd been the next best thing to comatose for the past several hours. They got up, one by one, and headed out of the garage, calling vague goodbyes to their coworkers as if it were a regular day.

The only thing different, as far as Thea could tell, was the glassy look in their eyes and the way they didn't seem to realize anything was amiss. They were clearly still all under some sort of spell. Thea stood next to Ezra, watching them.

"Shouldn't we try to stop them?" she asked softly as the first of the wolves got on their bikes and headed down the street at a sensible pace.

"I don't see how," Ezra said on a gusty sigh. "But I do think we need to follow where they lead. The moon rises early tonight. We'll want to be wherever these guys end up in time to try to identify and stop the mage. He'll have to be nearby, right? In order to benefit the most from the bloodshed?"

"Yeah, he'll want to be right up close and personal," Thea confirmed. "Making others suffer is the kind of thing evil folks really get off on."

"Then, that's where we need to be." He didn't look too happy about it, but she was glad he was including her in his plans. She would've been very upset if her new mate didn't understand that seeing this through was something she had to do for herself, for her mate, for the wolves, and ultimately, for a full recovery from the ordeal she'd been through.

Thea realized the three bear brothers had come up to stand next to them as they spoke. All were watching the departing wolves. By ones and twos, the wolves were heading out.

"We'll lock up here, and then, we should probably follow before the last one leaves," King said.

"Definitely," Ezra replied.

"Any news on the cavalry?" Ace asked quietly.

Ezra frowned. "We can't count on any backup."

"Looks like we'll have to do this the hard way, then," King said, summing up all their thoughts.

They left soon after, Ezra and Ace coordinating their approach and positioning. Ezra and Thea rode side by side, following the highest-ranking wolf of those who'd been in the garage.

The brothers spread out, following other clusters of wolves who all seemed to be heading in the same direction, though they took various routes through town. Each took a slightly different path, making the exodus look almost random.

When they reached the open road, however, it was clear they were all going the same way. Thea, Ezra, and the other bears followed along like they were part of the Pack, and nobody even seemed to notice them. When they turned off onto a dirt road, the bears held back a bit, wanting to be among the last to arrive, so they could hide their presence as long as possible since it was likely the mage who was causing all of this was watching every arrival at their chosen killing field.

"If we go in too early," Ezra had reasoned when they'd been planning this, "the mage could just scatter them all and try again later. We'll only have one shot at taking the bastard by surprise."

Thea had agreed, and so had the other bears, even though it was a little riskier this way for the wolves. They might start right in on the battle, and then, it would be harder to stop, but there was no elegant way to do this. Someone was going to get hurt no matter what. Thea just hoped it was the mage and not the shifters.

CHAPTER TEN

Ezra wasn't thrilled that Thea was in the danger zone, but he knew she needed to be here. He knew she needed this—to face her worst fears—to heal from what had been done to her. He didn't like it, but he understood the need.

He was so damned proud of how far she'd already come. She was a strong woman in every way. Her bear had bounced back and was mightier than it had been before. His Thea was something else, and he loved everything about her. Including her fierce spirit that refused to be cowed.

They approached the natural depression in the earth where the wolves were gathering cautiously. There was a shallow basin topped by a rocky ridge. A perfect place for a showdown if you wanted it contained and hidden from easy view by stray passing humans.

Ezra stopped his bike on the path that was well-worn by the passage of so many of the wolves and evaluated the situation. Thea stopped next to him, and Ace came up alongside a moment later.

"This looks like the place," Ezra said, taking a good hard look around.

There was more than one path that led into the crater, and it was clear the White Oaks wolves had come by another route. They were already there and waiting as the local wolf Pack arrived. Bikes had been left scattered all over the higher ground, and the wolves had arrayed themselves around the bowl in the earth—each taking half the roughly circular depression for their side. Like opposing armies waiting for the charge.

"King and Jack are coming in from either side," Ace reported. "But I have to say, this looks bad. Really bad."

Ezra nodded, watching everything, trying to figure out where the mage was hiding. Beside him, Thea stiffened, and he went instantly on alert.

"What is it?" he asked her quietly, not wanting to draw attention to them.

"You know that feeling you get when something rubs your fur the wrong way?" She was looking out over the assembled werewolves who all had that glassy, zombified look in their eyes again. "The mage is close."

"I don't see the local Alpha yet," Ace murmured from Ezra's other side. "Wait, there he is…and oh, shit. Here comes trouble."

Ezra looked to where Chase Rivers was arriving at the circle from the entrance just off to the left of where Ezra and company watched. And he wasn't alone. Chase stopped his bike and let a woman off the back. She was smiling, and her eyes definitely weren't glassy. In fact, she looked downright triumphant.

"It's her," Thea whispered at his side. "She's the mage."

Well, hell. Ezra hadn't really expected they'd be fighting a female magic user, but he shouldn't have been so surprised. Women could be just as vicious as men when their hearts had turned to evil. He'd seen it before.

"The Alpha's girlfriend?" Ace asked, incredulous. "I mean, we all thought she was a bitch of the first order, but we didn't think she was evil," he went on. "Then again, Jack never liked her, but he couldn't explain why. Little bro was right to stay away from her the few times she showed her face at the garage since we've been here."

"She came to the garage?" Ezra asked quietly, the pieces beginning to fall into place in his mind.

"Yeah. She went into private meetings with Frank a few times. We all thought it was strange, but we didn't know what to make of it. Her name is Sarella. At least, that's what she goes by. I figured it was a stripper name or something."

"Might be her last name. Mages seem to be known by their family names," Thea put in quietly. As the woman turned, and Thea got her first good look at Sarella's face, she gasped and put her hand on Ezra's forearm. "I've seen her before," she whispered, her face pale. "She came to the basement a couple of times. I think she was learning from Bolivar. He was training her. And sleeping with her. At least for a little while."

"You okay?" Ezra forgot everything, concentrating on Thea. As he watched, her face regained color, and her shoulders straightened, a firm resolve coming into her eyes as she met his gaze.

"I'm good. *This* is good. We can stop another one of those evil bastards and prevent this carnage," she told him, her voice low, but strong. "And I can get a little of my own back. That bitch bled me and laughed." Thea's eyes narrowed as she zeroed in on her prey standing some fifty yards distant. "Now, it's my turn."

Around them, the werewolves finished assembling and now faced each other like two opposing armies waiting for the signal to charge. The sorceress raised her arms, watching from the rim of the crater, and the zombie stares of the men and women all around changed from quiescent to angry as if someone had flipped a switch.

And, in fact, someone had. That sorceress was orchestrating this like a conductor in front of her orchestra, only they weren't going to make music. No, this group was going to make war. Bloodshed. Violence and probably death. All to power the woman who held them in thrall.

But not if Ezra could help it.

He wasn't sure how, exactly, this was going to go down yet, but he knew one thing for certain. He was going to put a stop to it, one way or another.

Thea watched the woman, remembering more and more about their past encounters. Thea had been in bear form each time the other woman had come, if she remembered correctly. Chances were Sarella wouldn't recognize Thea immediately, which meant she could probably get closer to the sorceress without her noticing.

"I'm going to position myself closer to her," Thea told Ezra as she got off her bike.

He reached out and put his hand on her forearm, halting her gently. "Are you sure?"

"Yeah, I'm sure." Thea didn't really have the words to explain why she knew what she had to do here, she just trusted that Ezra would understand.

He looked into her eyes then nodded at whatever he saw there and let her go. Thea moved off slowly, trying to keep behind the cover of the still-moving latecomers to the party, using the wolves as camouflage as she inched her way closer to Sarella.

She felt more than saw Ezra doing the same.

She was aware of the werewolves growing more restless as their two Alphas made their way down into the center of the natural amphitheater from opposing sides. They were dropping clothing as they went until they faced each other, chests bare, pants the only thing left to let fall when they shifted into their wolf forms for battle.

Not bad-looking males. In fact, if she'd still been single, she might've looked a little harder at the muscular men on parade, but her main focus was the sorceress. A protégé of Bolivar's, this woman was evil through and through. In a way, that made all of this easier for Thea. There was no doubt about the enemy, and if they managed to kill Sarella, so much the better. The world could only be better off without her in it.

Sarella raised her hands again, and based on the scene below, Thea figured this would be the start of the brawl. Thea wouldn't give her the chance.

"Remember me?" Thea asked, walking boldly forward, until she was only ten feet or so from Sarella.

The sorceress paused, seemingly surprised by Thea's presence.

"Who are you? Why are you here? This is a private meeting," Sarella said in a haughty tone that Thea remembered.

"Private battle, you mean," Thea muttered, just loud enough for the woman to hear. "So, you really don't remember me?"

"Should I?"

Was Sarella looking down her nose at Thea? No way. She truly was. Thea just shook her head.

"Considering I killed your pal, Bolivar, you probably should," Thea fibbed a little, wanting to see the other woman's reaction.

"You—?" Sarella seemed shocked by Thea's claim. And, yes, it was clear she knew exactly who Bolivar was, so Thea's memories were confirmed. This was his little bloodthirsty plaything. "Bolivar's dead?"

"You didn't know?" Thea hadn't expected that, but perhaps communications between evil mages wasn't as good as she'd thought.

Sarella moved fast to shoot a loosely concocted bolt of dull red energy at Thea. Her reflexes only marginally slower than her bear form, Thea ducked, and the mage fire just skimmed over her back, doing no damage. It hadn't missed her. It had slid away from her—as it would have slid off her fur if she'd been in bear form.

There was a reason only the most powerful mages dared to fuck around with bears. They were more magical than most shifters, and it was much harder to subdue them, both physically and magically. Most spells bounced right off—

unless the bear was already weakened, as Thea had been in Bolivar's basement.

"What are you?" Sarella all but shrieked.

"You really don't know?" Thea said, standing tall in front of the other woman once more and walking slowly closer, closing the gap between them.

The wolves around started to shift shape, and a few formed a ring of protection around Sarella, at her direction. She was waving her arms around again, causing all sorts of unrest around the circular depression in the earth. Down below, the two Alphas began circling each other, preparing to engage. Along either side, the armies began to prepare, as well, growling low in their throats, clearly agitated beyond all reason. Several shifted into their wolf form, their clothing discarded on the sides of the hill as they kicked their hind legs free of their pants.

Thea didn't let any of that distract her. She was peripherally aware of the other bears moving deeper into the bowl and Ezra somewhere behind and below her, but she wanted the mage. She wanted to end Sarella and her control over these poor wolves.

Thea might have to hurt a few to get to her goal, but she'd try to be as gentle as possible with the wolves. The mage? Not so much.

Ezra was torn. He wanted to help Thea, but he knew he had to let her stand on her own two—or maybe four—feet. The best way he could help her now, he decided, was to limit the amount of blood shed by the werewolves. The less power they funneled up to that sorceress, the better.

To that end, Ezra jumped into the middle of the circle, putting himself between the two werewolf Alphas, hoping to stop this before it really got a chance to get going. So far, they'd only been posturing. Circling each other, looking for an opening or some kind of weakness to exploit.

They were pretty evenly matched. Both in their prime and well-built for combat. If this had been a friendly contest, it might've been interesting to see how it ended, but this wasn't friendly. This wasn't even sane. Both were clearly under Sarella's control and not doing this of their own free will. That made this a disgusting display, worthy only of scorn. But it wasn't really their fault, Ezra knew. Magic was sometimes very hard to fight.

"Alphas," Ezra shouted to be heard above the growling. "This fight isn't yours. You're being manipulated by a *Venifucus* mage."

While Ezra wasn't one hundred percent certain of Sarella's *Venifucus* ties, it was a pretty good bet that she was in league with that ancient order of evil. Perhaps the word alone would help jog some of these wolves to their senses. He scanned the slope, looking for anyone who might be coming out of the bespelled state and found only one man looking confused.

Praise the Goddess, it was Arch. If he let loose with all his skill and knowledge of combat, Goddess help anyone who got in his way. All wolves were dangerous, but Arch Hanson was in a league of his own. If they could keep him from fighting, they could prevent a lot of damage.

"Sarella has you all under her spell," Ezra went on, keeping one eye on the combatants he stood between and another on the little drama taking place farther up the hill where Thea was facing off with Sarella. Ezra sent a prayer heavenward that Thea would be all right.

As if Thea had heard, she let out a piercing wolf whistle that made everyone near her cringe back a bit. It was loud and jolting, and it got everyone's attention.

"Hey, wolves!" Thea shouted to be heard throughout the natural amphitheater. "This bitch Sarella is in league with evil. She hurt me and stole some of my power. I'm here to get it back. Don't feed her evil by hurting each other for her pleasure. You're being used!"

Thea staggered as Sarella sent another mage bolt at her back. It didn't hurt Thea, but it definitely got her attention. Thea turned on Sarella and growled. A bear growl that made it clear she was nothing like these wolves. Ezra felt so proud of her in that moment. Worried for her, too, but so damned proud.

Thea turned back toward Sarella, annoyed by the cheap shot the bitch had taken at her back. It had hurt a bit, but Thea was much stronger now than she'd been the last time they'd met. This time, it would be Sarella who ended up bleeding.

"You shouldn't have done that," Thea warned the other woman.

"Why not? You're just a filthy animal," Sarella spat.

"Wrong," Thea told her, shaking her head. "I'm a fucking bear, Sarella. The bear you once bled is now going to make you bleed. Remember me now?"

And, with a roar, Thea allowed her bear to come over her. Her clothes shredded, but she didn't care. The bear wanted out, now. It wanted revenge on the woman who had hurt her so badly. It wanted justice.

Sarella gaped and seemed to order her wolves to attack, but Thea in bear form sent them all flying. She tried to swat them away so that none would be permanently hurt, but she couldn't be sure. A couple of the faster wolves tried to bite her, but Thea was having none of it. They all got swatted, and if they came back, they got swatted again. Eventually, they learned their lesson, and it was just Thea and Sarella, facing each other.

Thea's bear was in a rage, remembering what it had suffered at this woman's hands. But there was no cage around Thea to protect Sarella this time. Sarella tried to send her muddy red mage fire at Thea, but it all just slid right off Thea's fur while her righteous anger carried her forward. Sarella raised her arms to throw even more magic at Thea, but she was too close now.

Thea pounced, taking the sorceress down to the ground, her claws biting into the woman's shoulders, making her bleed. The rich, coppery scent of Sarella's blood brought a deep sense of satisfaction to Thea's bear half. Finally, she was getting a little of her own back, and this woman—this sorceress—would never hurt her again.

Down below, Sarella's spells began to falter as Thea confronted the sorceress above. Ezra watched closely as the wolves began to come awake, some looking around in horror and disbelief as if waking from a nightmare.

The two Alpha stopped in their tracks and just looked at each other.

"What the fuck is going on here?" Chase Rivers asked as he shook his head as if to clear it.

"Magic," Arch Hanson spat, coming up to stand next to his nephew, Brock, the White Oaks Alpha. "We've all been bamboozled and bespelled, but our bear friends stepped up where we dropped the ball. Can we help now?" Arch offered, looking directly at Ezra then switching his gaze to the side of the hill where Thea, in bear form, had Sarella trapped beneath her claws.

Ezra signaled the bear brothers—who were all in bear form—to close in on Thea's position, now that the wolves seemed to have shaken off the spell. Ezra was already climbing the side of the hill, as well.

"Just stand down," Ezra called back to the wolves. "We'll take care of the mage."

Ezra reached the two women just as Thea reared up, away from a black blade that gleamed dully in the night air. It reeked of evil—and blood. That had to be the mage's athame, and Ezra would be damned if he'd let it hurt Thea ever again.

He dove for the woman, reaching out with both hands to take her wrists and keep the blade away from Thea. His momentum took the woman back to the ground, and they rolled a bit, somehow ending up with Ezra rolling free and jumping up to face the woman.

But Sarella didn't get up. In fact, the smell of blood only became stronger. And then, he realized...

She'd stabbed herself with her own blade in the tussle. Right through the heart—if she actually had one.

Sarella was dead.
And the wolves were freed.

CHAPTER ELEVEN

Many of the werewolves just sank to the ground wherever they stood, those in their fur changed back to human form and began searching for their discarded clothes and shrugging into them. Those who had remained in human form looked bewildered and seemed to be seeking the comfort of their fellow Pack mates.

Ezra went over to Thea and just held out his arms, letting her choose whether or not to come to him. He was okay with whatever she wanted to do. She was a full grown, badass grizzly bear, and he loved every inch of her furry little self. Of course, she was *little* only in relation to him.

His bear was larger than hers, so to him, she was petite, while to everyone else, she was one titan of a mama bear. He loved that. He loved that everyone else would give her a wide berth, but she was his perfect match. She would never have reason to fear him in either of his forms, because she was as fierce and not-to-be-trifled-with as he was.

Thea came up to him and nestled close to his side. He ran his hands over her soft fur and reveled in the feel of his mate, safe, sound, and whole. He knelt in front of her to look into her eyes.

"You're amazing, Thea. Gorgeous and strong, and all mine," he whispered for her ears alone.

She put her massive, furry head over his shoulder, and then, he felt the tickle of magic as she turned back into her human form, hugging him with all her might. She was luscious and naked, but everyone around was a shifter. Nakedness was no big deal among their people. Still, she'd need some sort of covering to drive back into town. Ezra would deal with that in a minute. For now, he just held her through the shakes that came after the confrontation.

Thea wasn't a hardened soldier. She wasn't used to this kind of thing. Still, she'd handled the problem like a pro and had come out the victor. Her actions had brought about the end of an evil person who had held not just one, but two entire wolf Packs in thrall and ready to do mayhem to each other. Thea had helped save many wolf lives this night, and if she was a little shaky after the fact, nobody would think less of her for it.

On the contrary, the fact that she didn't take the death of the sorceress in stride made the wolves respect her more. They'd heard what she'd said to Sarella, even in their zombie states. They might not have understood the full import as it had happened, but they knew what Thea had been saying now, and Ezra saw many of the wolves looking at them with approval, some with compassion, others with awe.

Not every member of the Packs that had been about to fight were actual fighters. There were many women and younger Pack members present on these hillsides. Many that wouldn't have been engaged in warfare in the normal course of business. Those were the one who wore looks of horror at what had been about to happen. Non-dominant wolves and downright submissive wolves who would normally have been protected from this sort of confrontation.

Ezra noted the two Alphas going around to their people, speaking quietly and offering comfort. Nobody approached Thea and Ezra, though. The three bear brothers stood guard around them, their tall forms blocking the way even if any of the wolves had gotten up the gumption to interrupt.

But the wolves were moving away, gathering around their respective Alphas, seeking comfort and a clue as to what was going on. All hint of hostility was gone, and Arch was acting as go-between among the older and more military-looking of the Pack's elders. Ezra thought that was a good sign.

"You guys okay?" Ace asked from beside Ezra. He was facing outward, watching the crowd below and the body of the dead sorceress rather than Ezra and his lady. Classy. And vigilant.

"We're good, right, Thea?" Ezra drew back to look into her eyes. She was still a little shaky but doing better with each passing minute. She smiled for him.

"Right," she told him. "But I ruined my clothes." They chuckled together, able to smile after the ordeal. They'd lived, and the bad guy was dead. That had to count for something.

"That's okay," he told her. "You're a knockout, no matter what form you wear. And I bet we can scrounge up something for you to cover up with for the ride back to the hotel." He spotted something over her shoulder. "Your shoes survived, at least."

Ezra looked up at Ace and gestured with his eyes. The other man went over and picked up the shoes Thea had worn, which had taken only minimal damage when she'd shifted to her bear form. Ace dusted them off and placed them down next to Thea, then he seemed to go into hunt mode.

The sorceress had ridden in behind the Southern Buttes Alpha, and she'd left some of her gear on his bike. Ace seemed to realize about the same time Ezra did that the other woman wouldn't be needing her fancy coat or the scarf she'd left behind anytime soon. Plus, there might be information in her clothing that they could use. Regardless of whether or not Thea wanted to wear the coat or scarf, they'd be taking it back with them when they left, for further examination.

Ace called to his youngest brother—the one who was

sensitive to magic—and asked Jack to sniff over the belongings of the dead sorceress. Wise precaution, Ezra thought. Jack nodded before Ace turned and brought the items back to Ezra.

Meanwhile, King went down to talk to the local wolf Alpha. When he came back, he went right back to the Alpha's bike and removed a set of saddlebags, handing them to Jack for a good going-over before he headed toward Ezra and Thea with them. King crouched down beside Ezra and emptied the bags, which were full of clothing.

"Chase said that this was all Sarella's, and we're welcome to it, if it'll help. He's a bit in shock and feeling a lot of guilt. I think we're going to have to talk to the man tomorrow, once this all sinks in," King said.

Ezra nodded. "We can get help for him, and the others, if we need to, but I think he'll bounce back. His Pack is strong and, aside from this incident, solid. Now that they've been badly burned once, they'll be more hesitant about who they let close in future."

While Ezra talked in low tones with King, Thea peeled back from him and started looking through the scraps of fabric. They were just clothes, as far as Ezra could see. Nothing dangerous, even if they had belonged to a madwoman.

Luckily, Thea was able to find a pair of stretchy yoga pants in the pile and a matching tank top. Both were black and both fit her like a second skin. Yowza.

The little white leather jacket fit over the stretchy black and looked amazing on Thea. For borrowed clothes, they fit like a glove. Nobody would ever know, looking at her now, that she was walking around in someone else's kit.

Everybody else who had shifted had gone back to human form and found something to put on, just in case their little party was found by any passing humans. They hadn't exactly hidden their trail here, but so far, it looked like they were going to get away with it, without any humans having seen anything.

When Ezra noticed Chase approaching Brock, holding out the hand of friendship, he realized everyone was holding their breath to see if the visiting Alpha would take issue with what had almost happened because of Chase's girlfriend. But Brock was a steady sort of fellow, and he took Chase's hand without hesitation, even pulling him in for a bro hug and some quiet words. Ezra noticed Arch nodding in approval from the background, as were several elders on either side.

When the Alphas broke apart, they walked together to where the bear shifters were safeguarding Sarella's body. Thea was keeping her distance, but Jack was right next to Sarella, keeping watch with his extra sharp magical senses.

"How can we thank you?" Brock asked simply, looking at all five bear shifters in turn but focusing especially on Thea.

"You saved us all a lot of bloodshed and sorrow," Chase added in a subdued tone. "If not for you, a large part of our Packs would be injured or dead by now." Murmurs of fear and agreement met the local Alpha's pronouncement.

"I'm just glad Thea was able to stop her," Ezra said, standing tall beside his mate. She really deserved all the credit here. If not for her, they would have had a hell of a time dealing with Sarella.

"You killed her?" Chase asked Thea, looking at the body of the woman he'd been sleeping with until now. Ezra knew there was a lot of regret in the other man's eyes, but he'd have to be one cold-hearted son of a bitch to not feel something now that the woman was dead.

"I'd have to take credit—or blame—for that," Ezra said, stepping in. "She had the knife pointed at Thea's belly. I dove for Sarella, grabbing for her hands, and we tumbled. In the tussle for the blade, it got turned around, and when we rolled, she took it to the chest," Ezra reported the way he'd been taught in the military. Just the facts. No excuses.

"You weren't intending for her to die?" Chase asked, proving that he wasn't as cold-hearted as he tried to portray. That was actually reassuring to Ezra.

"No. If we could have captured her, I would have escorted

her to the Lords myself. She might have been a good source for information about what our enemies are up to right now," Ezra said, honest as he could be with the man who had just had his love life turned on its ear.

Chase nodded solemnly. "I know I've been a fool, but I really liked her when we first met. I'm not sure when the brainwashing—or whatever you want to call it—started, but she seemed like such a nice girl before…" Chase swallowed hard. "It's going to take time," he said finally and turned away.

Ezra felt for the man. Brock put a comforting hand on Chase's shoulder, and the two werewolf Alphas walked away, back to their waiting Packs. Both Packs were intermingled now, friends again after a harrowing experience, Ezra was pleased to note.

By ones and twos, they began to head back to their bikes and then get on the road back to town. They'd arrived in a staggered fashion to avoid causing too much of a stir. They'd go back the same way.

Arch Hanson came up to the bears with a delegation of older wolves who all had that military bearing Ezra knew, from experience, was hard to shake. Arch looked at Ezra and then at the body of the fallen mage.

"Any plans on what to do with her?" Arch asked quietly.

"Not a one," Ezra replied. "Do you have any ideas?"

"Clint here is a local, and a fellow SEAL." Arch gestured to the burly werewolf standing to his right. "We can disappear her where she'll never be found, if that's all right. Is there anything special we need to do considering her magical past?"

"If you don't mind me tagging along, I can take care of that for you," Jack volunteered. Ezra nodded at the youngest brother, glad he'd stepped up.

"Jack's your man for magical stuff. He's got the best nose of all of us and not inconsiderable abilities of his own." Ezra endorsed the younger bear.

"Then, we'll be glad of his help," Arch said, nodding, as

did the other ex-military wolves with him. Then, Arch stepped up to Thea and took her hand in his. Ezra watched carefully, bristling at the nearness of any male to his mate. "Thank you, milady," Arch said softly. "Your bravery in standing up for us has not gone unnoticed. We owe you a blood debt, and we will never forget that. You have friends among the White Oaks and Southern Buttes Packs, now and forevermore."

Then, Arch leaned down and kissed the back of Thea's hand like some kind of medieval knight. Ezra watched, bemused, as Thea blushed. She seemed surprised by the attention but truly touched by the warrior wolf's words.

Arch turned and left her, moving to discuss logistics with his small group of ex-military wolves and Jack. Thea just shook her head as he left, meeting Ezra's gaze with a sort of shocked and amused expression on her lovely face. Ezra went to her and tugged her in for a quick hug.

"All right?" he asked. When she nodded, he shifted so that his arm was around her shoulders. "Ready to roll? I think these guys can handle the cleanup here."

"Yeah, I'm ready to leave this place and never come back," she said, her words dripping with post-battle exhaustion. After the adrenaline that must've been powering her moves throughout the confrontation, there was bound to be a bit of a letdown now that things were quieter.

Ezra walked, arm in arm, with Thea back to where they'd left their bikes and took a moment to just hold her before they took off. When they parted, they mounted their separate bikes and headed out, making their way back to town and their waiting hotel room.

Once back at the hotel, Thea stripped out of the borrowed clothes and put them in a plastic bag. She didn't want to see them ever again, but Ezra might want them for some reason, since they'd belonged to Sarella.

Sealing up the plastic bag as tight as she could, she put it in the farthest corner of the room. She didn't want to be reminded of that woman or her clothes for as long as she could manage it. Sure, the fallout of this day's work would take a long time to deal with, but Thea didn't really need the visual reminders on display every time she walked through the room.

Thea heard Ezra making a phone call and letting someone know that the cavalry was no longer needed. He had a large network of friends with very interesting skills, it seemed, which she thought was probably a very useful thing to have when you put yourself on the line as part of your daily work routine. He may call himself a troubleshooter, but he was more of a trouble-magnet.

Of course, there was no one better suited to deal with trouble when it found him. Ezra was one in a million. She'd respected him before, but after the action today, her admiration for his skills and acumen had only risen. He was hell on wheels when it counted and she was so blessed to have him in her life. He was a special man. A special bear.

As she listened for a moment, she could hear him giving a concise report of what had happened. She went about her business as he spent a few minutes explaining the action to whoever he had called, but Thea tuned him out after the first few moments. She had better things to do than rehash what she'd just lived through.

She marched herself straight into the shower and turned the water on as hot as she could stand it. She needed to wash off the stink of the battle. The stink of her own fear and sweat. The smell of Sarella's blood on her hands.

A hot shower would be a good start.

Ezra let Thea have a few minutes to herself, but he knew not to leave her alone too long. He had a few reports to file, and he could easily guess at the kind of emotional issues sweeping through Thea's mind.

He'd been in combat. Many times, in fact. He knew what it could be like after, and he hoped he could provide what Thea needed so that she wouldn't suffer damage to her own fierce spirit by what had happened tonight.

He vowed that he wouldn't let that happen. No how. No way. Thea was done being hurt if Ezra had anything to say about it.

He made a few, very necessary, phone calls. There were folks higher up the food chain who needed to know what had happened here, including his employers and even his contact close to the Lords of all Werefolk. The Lords were keeping track of all the strange happenings in their territory, which included the entirety of North America. It was one of their tasks to look for patterns in magical activity or threats to shifters in their domain and coordinate a response, if at all possible.

By the time Ezra had given his reports to the proper people who could do something useful with his information, he figured he'd left Thea alone long enough. He started stripping off his clothing on his way towards the bathroom. When he opened the door to what had become a steam box, he was barefoot and bare-chested. Whether he lost his pants and joined her under the steamy spray of water was up to Thea. He leaned up against the wall to the side of the enclosure and met her gaze through the foggy air.

"How are you doing, honey?" he asked quietly.

"I'm okay," she said, her voice thick with emotion. "It's hard to get clean."

Now that said more than the simple words used in the sentence. He knew that feeling. The stain of death on your soul that made it hard to feel truly clean.

"Do you want some help? I can scrub your back," he offered, smiling gently at his lover, his mate.

In answer, she pushed aside the clear curtain and invited him in. Ezra shucked his pants in a quick move and joined her under the near-scalding spray. He adjusted the water temperature to something a little lower than the *molten lava* setting she'd had it on and gathered her into his arms.

She was wet, and her skin was slippery against him, soap suds still lingering in places where she hadn't yet washed them away. And she was trembling.

That would never do. Ezra rocked her slick body against him, trying to impart some of his strength to her shaky limbs. He stroked his hand down her spine, trying to soothe her, and she responded to his touch, calming after a long while. At that point, he began to take care of her. He grabbed the soap and lathered her body again, making sure to get the spots she'd missed the first time and scrubbing her back like he'd promised, combining washing with a gentle massage.

She leaned back into him after a while, and he just held her, wrapping his arms around her middle and enjoying the sensation of her soft, wet body against his. He lowered his head, nuzzling her ear.

"You feeling better now?" he asked, his voice low in the echo chamber of the shower.

"Yeah. Thanks." She paused before continuing. "I didn't expect it to feel so bad...after. I mean, I felt triumphant at the time, and I'm glad I was able to overcome my fears and all, but it's not like I expected it to be now."

"That's because you have a conscience and you're a good person," he told her. "While you may have felt a thrill of exhilaration at the moment of triumph, you aren't the kind of soul who revels in death." He kissed her temple. "It had to be done, and it wasn't your fault. Fate decided Sarella's final moments. Neither of us intended to kill her. It just happened. And, because we are people of conscience, we'll think about it and wonder if there was something we could have done differently."

Thea turned in his arms to look up into his eyes. "I saw what happened with her and that knife. There was nothing you could've done differently, Ezra. She basically killed herself by not surrendering when she knew her plan was foiled. By continuing to fight and by pulling that knife on me, she sealed her own fate."

He knew his tender-hearted mate was saying this to make him feel better, but he'd long ago come to terms with the fog of war. Things happened. Things you couldn't control, didn't plan, and never expected. How you dealt with them after the action was what determined your path in life. If he hadn't been able to cope, he would've given up soldiering long ago and become a fisherman...or something even less confrontational.

"I'm glad you feel that way, Thea," he said quietly. "What you just said? It applies to you as well as me."

Thea's eyes widened, and then, she chuckled softly and shook her head. "You're a sly one, Ezra Tate."

He tapped one finger to his temple and returned her grin. "Always think a step ahead."

"Is that what they taught you in the military?" she asked, almost purring.

Ezra took her playfulness as a good sign that she was coming out of the battle shock. He stepped up his game, leaning in to kiss her, taking his time about it.

When Ezra kissed her like that, time and space stood still. They were the only two beings in the universe, and soon, it would be hard to tell where she started and he left off. She loved the way he could make her forget everything but him. Her mate.

Maybe that's what mates were supposed to do? She'd bet the Mother of All knew exactly what She was doing when she matched up certain souls. In her case, Ezra had seen her at her absolute worst. And he was starting to see her at times when she was proud of the woman she had become out of her ordeal. Maybe, as they traveled the path of life together, he'd get to see her when she'd finished evolving into...whatever it was she was now becoming.

She still wasn't exactly sure what she was. She'd been a warrior tonight, but it didn't feel good after the fact. Maybe that wasn't her path. But she'd certainly felt good helping Ezra track down the problem here in South Dakota. Maybe she would be able to help him in his investigations, if he kept working as a troubleshooter.

There were so many question marks about the future.

They hadn't really discussed it at all yet, but she was confident they'd figure it out. At the moment, all she really could concentrate on was Ezra. Kissing her. Making her feel not-alone in the universe. Making her feel…loved.

She welcomed him when he pushed her up against the cool tile of the shower. After the near-scalding temperatures she'd started out with, the slick tile felt good against her back. And it was slippery, so when he lifted her up with one strong hand under her buttocks, she slid happily up the wall in defiance of gravity.

When he probed at her entrance with his hard cock, she was ready and waiting, wanting him inside with no further preliminaries. Tonight was about raw emotion, not finesse. She didn't have time or patience for finesse. They'd do that later. Much later.

For now, she wanted him inside her, fucking her in the most primal way. Man to woman, need to need. Life to life. Love to love.

They had survived the test and come out the victors. They had vanquished their enemy and saved a lot of souls from pain and bloodshed. They'd done good. But this moment was just for them. Alone. Two souls, becoming one.

Ezra pushed inside as she held his gaze, loving him silently, yearning for the moment when they would be complete, yet not wanting to rush to the culmination of this experience. It was too powerful. Too raw emotionally. Too honest to let pass too soon.

He seated himself, and they just stayed there for a long moment, looking deep into each other's eyes. All traces of mirth were gone. This was just them. Bare. Naked in every way. Unrefined emotion billowing through their spirits and buffeting each other, protecting each other when they finally found the sync between their souls.

Then, he began to move within her, and they found a new synchronization. A new rhythm that was theirs alone in all the universe. Ezra pushed, and Thea accepted for a long while until it felt like they were straining together toward some unreachable knowledge that would reveal all the secrets of existence, just for them.

Thea growled, and Ezra answered, from deep in his throat. Their animal spirits were present and approved of their human sides' actions. The animals didn't understand some human concepts, but they grasped devotion and the natural perfection that Thea and Ezra, together, created and refined. Their animal instincts had recognized it well before their human sides, when Thea's bear had fought to survive because Ezra was there, holding a promise of this moment in his soul, as he'd held her tortured body in his arms.

She'd have known way back then, if she'd been able to hear the thoughts of her splintered bear half, that they would come to this moment out of time. This communion of souls. This commitment of hearts.

She exploded in sensation as Ezra shouted her name, his growls driving her own passions higher. She felt the rumble of his bear under his skin, the sound vibrating against her sensitized skin. It was glorious.

The climax went on and on, them straining together while the water kept pulsing down around them, steam wafting through the air like the clouds in the sky. She was floating on them, held suspended by Ezra's strong arms and the wall behind her.

She never wanted to move again. She could die happy, right here in the hotel room shower.

But Ezra wouldn't let her do anything of the kind. After long, long moments of bliss, he lifted slightly away, bending his head slightly to kiss her. Deep, drugging kisses. Kisses of thanks. Kisses of joy. Kisses of the commitment of one heart to another that said, without words, that this... This was forever.

He lifted her off him and out of the shower, depositing her bare ass on the stone countertop next to the sink. Luckily, it was covered with a towel she'd left out, or she would've jumped at the cold stone on her overheated skin. The tile in the shower stall had been one thing while her passions were riding high, but in the aftermath, she was feeling a bit more sensitive.

Ezra dried her off, using another of the fluffy towels provided by the hotel. He wrapped one around her hair and squeezed a lot of the moisture out. She'd scrubbed her scalp hard before he'd joined her and used the entire little bottle of shampoo provided by the hotel. They'd have to get more if they stayed, but she couldn't regret her cleaning binge. She felt a lot better and knew that not a single molecule of Sarella's blood was left on her person. That was important.

Her claws had sunk deep into the sorceress's skin, and when Thea had shifted back, that meant her nails and fingers had been bloody. She'd wiped it off as best she could, but Thea hadn't felt that her hands were really clean until she'd scrubbed at them under the hot water with loads of soap.

Ezra dried his own stunning body with a lot less care than he showed her. Still, she felt herself salivating as he drew a damp towel over his chest and muscular torso. She wanted to lick the moisture off his body, but her muscles were limp. He'd loved her into the next incarnation, and though her spirit was willing for more, her flesh had experienced about all it had the energy for just at that moment.

She didn't protest when Ezra picked her up in his strong arms and walked, naked, with her into his bedroom. He deposited her on his bed and came down next to her, tucking them both under the covers. He drew her into his arms and spooned her close. She felt absolutely wonderful. And tired.

"Sleep, honey. We'll talk about everything in the morning. Right now, we both need some rest," he whispered against her ear, nibbling on the lobe lightly, as if he couldn't help himself.

She smiled, even as sleep started to steal over her senses. "You're a good mate, Ezra."

CHAPTER TWELVE

When Ezra arrived at the garage the next morning, he found a very contrite Frank waiting for him. Thea was at Ezra's side, where she belonged, as he followed the old wolf into his office. Ezra was somewhat surprised that Frank wasn't a little more resistant to the idea that Ezra wanted to meet with him alone. As far as Ezra knew, nobody in this town except for the other bears knew that he worked for Trevor and Beth.

But Frank seemed to give every indication of a man who'd been called on the carpet by his boss. How did he know? Or perhaps he had some different idea of what Ezra really wanted? Ezra shook his head as the garage manager closed the door behind Thea then came around and took a seat behind his cluttered desk.

"Frank, do you know why I'm here?" Ezra asked, figuring he'd have to set a few things straight before this interview could progress.

"Because I was fooled by that witch," Frank said, his voice rising almost to a wailing howl as he lowered his shaking head into his hands. "I'm so sorry."

Ezra looked over at Thea. This would never do.

"Hang on a minute, Frank." Ezra tried to calm the other man, but it seemed no use.

Thea reached across the desk and touched one of Frank's arms. That seemed to jolt him out of his misery. He looked up at Thea and met her gaze.

"Frank, Ezra works for the people who own this garage. It's why he came to town in the first place," she told Frank softly.

Frank's eyes widened, and he turned to look at Ezra, his gaze finally clear. "You do?"

Ezra nodded. "I'm a troubleshooter for the corporation that owns this garage, among other things, and I've been traveling around, trying to clean up certain operations that have been involved in illegal or immoral activities. The new ownership wants everything legal and above board. I came here because of the drug smuggling."

Frank began to shake his head again. "I'm so sorry." This was one defeated werewolf. Ezra was very much afraid that last night's revelations had all been too much for Frank. They'd broken him. "That pretty lady had me wrapped around her finger, and I did whatever she wanted. The money from the smuggling went to her. I have all the information here." Frank stood and went over to a filing cabinet against the wall. He brought back a stack of folders and a set of ledger books, handing them to Ezra. "I see now it was wrong, but I just...didn't...at the time."

"It's likely that she used magic on you," Thea told Frank gently.

She was a lot better at handling the fragile old werewolf than Ezra would have been. It was good to have her here, helping. Normally, by now, Ezra would've had someone like Frank gibbering and anything he said would've been useless until he calmed down.

Thea's words seemed to bring the old guy hope. His eyes widened as if he hadn't thought that far ahead, and he seemed to sit up a little straighter when he retook his seat at the desk.

"Regardless of how, this happened on my watch, and I take responsibility. I think it's time I hung up my wrench regardless. I haven't done much of the actual work around here in years. The younger men are the mechanics now. They need a younger boss who understands the computerized engine parts. I respectfully resign," Frank said with the shreds of his dignity gathered close.

Ezra nodded gravely. "While I know you did a good job with this place for many years, I will accept your resignation on behalf of my employer. I'm sorry, Frank, but we need someone in charge here that's above reproach."

Frank stood, nodded once and turned to leave. "I live in town. If you need me for anything—or to answer for what's happened here on my watch, you know where to find me. I'm not leaving. Not running. I'll answer for my actions, if you deem it necessary."

"I respect that, Frank," Ezra said, impressed by the old timer's resolute attitude. "Thank you."

Unless he found something Frank was truly culpable for, Ezra didn't think there would ever be any need to take him up on that offer. Ezra was in favor—especially in light of the magical interference here—to let bygones be bygones and just start fresh with new management. That was if he could convince the man he had in mind for the job to give it a try.

But that would come later. For now, he had work to do.

Thea was a great help in going through the books and files. She had a good nose for faulty accounting and managed to find a few places in the cooked books where money had been laundered and otherwise hidden from legitimate channels. Not only was the shop being used as a way station for drug shipments making their way northward to Canada, but it was also laundering money for the same endeavor.

"It looks like this all started about two years ago, when there's a notation of Sarella first showing up in the records," Thea said about an hour later. She and Ezra had taken over the office and were doing their best to untangle the records. "It looks like she was a regular visitor, coming through town for about two weeks each month. At least, as far as I can tell from this."

"We should ask Chase," Ezra said, his mouth forming a grim line. He hated to call the local Alpha on the carpet so soon after his rude awakening, but it couldn't be helped. This mess needed cleaning up, and the sooner, the better.

Ezra got up and leaned out the office door. The mechanics were hard at work. They'd all seen Frank leave, but they still had clients to serve and work to do. Ezra was glad to see them all back at work today. He'd sort through their involvement, one by one, but for now, the fact that they'd all shown up for work boded well for them. To Ezra, that meant that they probably hadn't been cooperating with Sarella out of their own volition, but he'd judge each case on its own merits once he had all the evidence sorted out.

"Anybody know where Chase is likely to be this time of day?" Ezra asked the group of wolves gathered in the nearest repair bay.

"Pool hall, most likely," one of the younger men answered.

"You got a number I could call? I need to talk with him," Ezra said in what he hoped was a reasonable tone. No sense making the werewolves think Ezra was going after their Alpha now.

"Sure," the same young man answered, moving closer and reciting the phone number from memory.

Ezra thanked him and ducked back into the office, closing the door behind him. He used the office phone to dial the number. It was answered on the third ring by a female voice. Ezra asked for Chase and was told to hold. Less than a minute later, Chase came on the line. Sounding much subdued, the Alpha offered to come by the garage so they could discuss matters, and Ezra rang off, looking at the phone's handset in puzzlement before replacing it back into the cradle on the desk.

"How did he sound?" Thea asked as she came back into the room holding two steaming cups of coffee.

She'd left while Ezra had made the phone call, to grab refreshments for them both. Ezra accepted the cup of coffee she offered him, as well as the lingering kiss that came along with it. He wouldn't mind getting used to having her around. No, not at all. It was nice to have someone to share the burdens of life and, now, even his work with. He wondered if Beth and Trevor would considering making Thea's position official so that she could be paid for her efforts. He made a mental note to broach the subject when he spoke to them next.

"Sort of defeated." He frowned. "But he's coming over, which is a good first step on the road to recovery."

Chase arrived a short while later and came straight into the office. Thea thought he looked sad and kind of worn out. She wasn't surprised. He'd been closest to Sarella and had probably been so deeply under her spell he hadn't had a clue what was going on. He might even have believed Sarella was his mate or something, which had to be hard for him now that she'd been exposed for the evil bitch she was.

What followed was one of the saddest interviews Thea had ever witnessed. Chase wasn't just down in the dumps, he blamed himself for everything that had happened. It took Ezra some time to talk the man around into discussing just the facts and not his own feelings of guilt and remorse, but somehow, Ezra managed it and the picture soon became clear.

Sarella had come into town about two years ago and immediately set out to bedazzle the werewolf Alpha. She'd played hard to get at first and, for a long while after, dangled herself in front of him, then retreating on one of her many business trips. Her story was that she was a regional sales rep for some big company, and this town was just one of several on her route.

She came and went with frequency, never really on a specific schedule. She'd stay for a week or two sometimes, only a day or two others. Whenever she was in town, she was sure to sashay into the pool hall to tease poor Chase until, eventually, she had him panting after her. At that point, he was probably fully under her spell.

She also visited the garage each time she was in town, dropping off or picking up shipments of drugs or money, or both. The drug running operation had already been in place for a while, but Sarella had become the new facilitator. Little by little, it seemed she'd put her whammy on the rest of the Pack until the culmination last night. It was pretty clear she'd been building up to last night for the past year or so.

She'd taken a great risk, expending a lot of her energy on that one operation, but she'd probably expected to gain a great deal more from the bloodshed she'd caused. Instead, she'd lost her gamble, thanks be to the Mother of All.

Thea got Chase to focus on the books, and starting with the most recent transactions, they were able to connect Sarella's appearances in town with happenings at the garage. Little by little, they worked out some of the coded notations next to each entry and decipher Frank's shorthand into something explicable. Chase turned out to be really good at reading the books, and Thea met Ezra's appraising gaze over the werewolf's head.

"Chase," Ezra said slowly, getting the Alpha wolf's attention. "Would you be willing to step in here and take over the garage for a while? Frank has resigned, and we're going to need someone strong enough to deal with any fallout Sarella's disappearance might cause."

Chase frowned. "What kind of fallout?"

"Well, it's possible Sarella's colleagues might come by to find out what's happened to their distribution line," Ezra told him.

"Mages?" Chase said immediately, a dark look coming over his face.

"Not necessarily," Thea jumped in, knowing what it was like to fear magical interference. "The mage that held me captive had mostly human allies." She saw the way Chase's eyes widened as she revealed a bit of her past to him. She felt it was important to let him know that he wasn't the first shifter to fall for a magic spell, and sadly, he probably wouldn't be the last. "I got caught up in a human trafficking ring where a group of criminals was kidnapping women and shipping them all over the country—and the world. Most of the women were regular humans, but a few that got caught up in the net were special. I was the only shifter, that I know of, but there were a few other slightly magical women being held captive by the same mage who had me. He was in league with the criminals, working for them in return for his pick of their catch."

She felt bile rise in her throat just thinking about it, but she pressed on. Chase needed to know that he wasn't alone in being taken in by a scoundrel.

"As far as I know, Bolivar, the mage who nearly killed me, was the only one involved with that ring. He had a few friends he brought in to show off his power base—his prisoners. Sarella was one of them. That's how I knew who she was when I saw her. Bolivar would bespell the other women prisoners to a glassy-eyed state like the one you and your wolves were under, but even though I felt the oppressive effects of the spell, I could still observe, and I remembered her." Thea felt stronger as she talked about this, which was surprising. Maybe last night's confrontation had helped her overcome even more than she'd thought. "But I definitely got the impression that each of the mages I saw were independent of each other. They were colleagues, of a sort, but they were each running their own scams. Bolivar worked alone. The only time we saw other mages was when he wanted to show us off and gloat."

"It's possible that Bolivar and Sarella were both *Venifucus* agents. If so, they might've been dispatched to these tasks. We know from intel reports from the Lords and other sources that the *Venifucus* is stretched thin right now. They've been working for years to bring their *Mater Priori*—the mother of their Order, Elspeth the Destroyer—back from her banishment to the farthest realms of existence. But, while they've been focusing on that, some of their number had to keep the wheels of commerce rolling and money coming in to support the communal endeavor. That's what Bolivar and Sarella were doing, I believe. Making money for the Order to spend on their main task," Ezra told them.

"Then, stopping them not only ends the evil they were doing, but also puts a hold on resources for the *Venifucus*," Chase said, nodding slowly.

"That's a really good thing," Thea added, "but it means that the *Venifucus* could possibly send another agent of theirs to look into matters here, or they might just leave it up to their non-magical allies."

"Yeah. Though, once they know that we know about an operation, there's really no sense in trying to start it back up again because it's pretty obvious we'll just send more folks here to stop it," Ezra put in. "My guess is that if anyone comes to check out what happened here, it'll be the non-magical sort. The *Venifucus* have other irons in the fire that we don't yet know about. Chances are, they'll tend to those and work on exploiting new avenues of revenue before fighting us for this one." Ezra leaned back in his chair. "But, either way, you're going to have to be vigilant. They're going to know something happened here and that Sarella has disappeared. They may never know what happened to her, but they'll be able to guess pretty easily. That can work in your favor. They won't want to risk another of their agents in a place and with people who have already made one of their mages disappear."

"There is that," Chase allowed, grimacing a bit. Then, he seemed to come to a decision. "Look. A lot of my people work here, and I want to help protect them. If bad business was happening out of this shop—and looking at these books, I'm certain it was—then it's my responsibility to clean it up. As long as the rest of the Pack still wants me to be Alpha."

That last was said with an air of sadness, and Thea looked at Ezra in concern.

"Is there some question about your continued leadership?" Ezra asked quietly.

Chase sighed hard. "Not really. They all say they want me to continue as Alpha, but to be honest, I'm having a crisis of conscience. I was completely bamboozled by that...by Sarella...and I'm not sure I'm fit to lead."

"Chase." Thea waited until the man looked her in the eye before continuing. "I've been where you are now. Even worse, I almost died at the hands of Sarella's friend, Bolivar. And I'm a grizzly. I had gone through life thinking nothing could ever get me down. Certainly not some piddly human mage. I might not have been very Alpha before my ordeal, but I've come back stronger than I ever was."

"All the women in my Pack are talking about the way you faced down Sarella last night, Thea," Chase told her. "I think they're starting a fan club for you." He chuckled softly, and she smiled. "But you're telling me you weren't always as badass as you were last night? I find it hard to believe."

Ezra reached over and covered her hand with his on the desk. "Believe it. I was the first one into the prison where she was being held. She was close to death and weaker than I've ever seen anyone who lived to tell the tale. She'd been tortured and bled. Her bear weakened to the point where it was almost gone."

Chase looked at her with surprise on his face. Surprise and admiration.

"That was just a few months ago," she told him gently. "You saw how far I've come in just a few months. I don't think this bad experience will keep you down long, Chase. If your people trust you to lead, you should trust them to know your heart. You were duped. So was I. We both have to get past that and move forward, stronger and wiser than we were before."

Chase looked at her as if he could discover the secrets of the universe from studying her face. Then, he looked at Ezra and shook his head.

"All right," he finally said. "I'll do what I can with this shop to bring it back to the righteous path. I'll look after my guys here and make sure, if anyone comes sniffing around, we learn all we can about them before sending them packing. I'll stay on until any threat of danger to my Pack is done and the garage is running on the straight and narrow again. After that, you can reevaluate, and if you want me to keep going—and if my Pack wants me to keep going—well, I'll think about it seriously. For now, I just want to clean up the problems in this town and within my Pack. Since they seemed to have been centered here, then this is where I'll be, fixing them."

Ezra nodded slowly. "Fair enough. I'll let the new owners know and get you on the payroll."

"Who are the new owners?" Chase asked. "I'd heard the original owner, a human named Zappo, sold out to some kind of West Coast based corporation years ago. The rumor was there were shifters involved, but nobody knew what kind. Zappo's went from being an all-human enterprise to being run by an old werewolf from my Pack who brought in his own crew—mostly youngsters he was mentoring as mechanics. I had the impression the buyers were from some kind of exotic species, but Frank said he didn't know exactly what the guy who hired him was. They only met once. Shifter, he said, but nothing he'd ever come across before. I assume the new people are the same, right?"

"Somewhat," Ezra said. "But also different." He sighed. "Since you'll be working for them, I think it's okay to say that the new owners are a newly mated couple living in Grizzly Cove," Ezra finally revealed in an even tone.

"That crazy bear shifter town in the Pacific Northwest? Man. I've heard rumors about that place, but I had no idea they were that big into business. I thought your kind didn't like to congregate into Packs," the werewolf observed.

"Normally, we like our space," Ezra confirmed, "but the guys who started the town are a special case. They all worked together for years in the military and have formed an extended family of sorts. I've seen it, and it really works. Great town. Nice people. They're just facing a few problems because they concentrated too much bear shifter magic in one place and earned the wrong sort of attention from a number of bad actors." Ezra frowned. "They're dealing with it, though. One of the bad guys was the man who had suborned a mer pod and basically stolen all their holdings on land by killing the merman who led the pod and forcing his widow into marriage. That was the fine piece of work who bought Zappo's and set up the drug distribution ring. After the folks in Grizzly Cove dealt with him, the business empire was turned over to its rightful heir, a mermaid who had mated one of the bear shifters there. They're running things together, and they hired me to clean up the illegal activities her stepfather had set up."

"You're kidding, right? Mermaids? I mean, I can see them on the coast, but here in South Dakota?" Chase looked bemused.

"Yeah, I know," Ezra agreed with him. "It gets even weirder. The guy who did all that? He was a shark shifter."

"No way," Chase exclaimed, shaking his head. "I never even heard of such a thing."

"Apparently, they exist. They're kind of rare, of course, but they do exist. The guy who was using Zappo's to smuggle drugs was a shark—figuratively and literally. He had his fins in the human trafficking ring, too. That's how I got involved and how I first met Thea," Ezra replied.

"That is some weird shit," Chase said, looking around the office. "I thought shifter but had no idea the owners were water-based. It's unexpected, especially at this elevation."

"Well, the new owners are half-and-half and trying to restore the assorted businesses in their portfolio to the right path. That's my job, so if you encounter anything you can't handle or that you think someone else needs to know about, you can always call me," Ezra told him.

They spent the rest of the morning going over the books. Thea thought Chase was looking a bit lighter in spirit as the day progressed. She hadn't shared her story easily, but she sensed that it had done some good in Chase's case.

Chase invited them to join him for lunch at the restaurant next to the pool hall, which was a base, of sorts, for his Pack.

He filled them in on the basic operations of the Pack while they ate, and they learned that the Pack owned not only the pool hall, but also the restaurant where they were enjoying a hearty lunch. Between the two businesses, they were able to employ many of the younger Pack members who didn't want to pursue higher education, have existing family businesses that could support them, or want to start businesses of their own.

It was clear that Chase cared for his Pack. They were his extended family, and he was a caring Alpha who wanted the best for his people.

"You know, if you get the garage back in shape, I'm pretty sure the new owners would be willing to consider a partnership with your Pack," Ezra said toward the end of the meal. "It's something to think about for the future, if you want to expand your Pack's holdings and build ties with other shifter groups. You've got a good start on building a financial base for your Pack already. There's no reason you couldn't expand a bit. Make things even more secure for your people."

Chase seemed surprised but pleased by the idea. "That's definitely something to think about," he answered, like a true diplomat.

Thea had to smile. Chase had come a long way from the nearly broken man who had entered the garage just a few hours ago. She felt confident that he'd be fine, given something constructive to do and time to get over what had to have been an emotional blow.

CHAPTER THIRTEEN

Ezra and Thea spent a few more days in town, going through the books and setting things to rights. By the time the rally was breaking up, they were about ready to get on the road, too. They stayed an extra day to say farewell to the bear brothers, who had jobs waiting for them back in Phoenix. They hinted things about their boss that would have to be seen to be believed, but Ezra didn't pry. He figured they'd tell him if he needed to know. He trusted all three of them enough to believe that.

Chase was coming along nicely, and he'd made amends with the visiting White Oaks Pack. Ezra had asked Arch Hanson to stay on in South Dakota for a few weeks, to act as a special troubleshooter should any of the drug runners come to call. He'd cleared the temporary position with Trevor, who was absolutely thrilled to have someone of Arch's reputation on board to help, should it become necessary.

So, when the rest of the White Oaks Pack headed home to Iowa, Arch stayed on at the garage. Trevor and Beth were footing the bill for a small apartment nearby and a generous expense account, as well as a decent salary. Ezra privately thought that Trevor was trying to lure Arch out of retirement and have him sign on full-time as a second troubleshooter, but the werewolf would need convincing, Ezra was sure.

Still, it would be nice to have help. Beth's stepfather had really fouled a lot of things up during the time he'd had control over Beth's inheritance. There were a lot of businesses still on Ezra's list to check out and fix up, but for now, he'd been told to go back to Grizzly Cove for a full debrief. That was a relief, because Ezra really wanted to show Thea the town and see what she thought of it. If she was amenable, he thought they just might be able to build a little place on the edge of town and settle down among their own kind.

It would make a great base of operations, even if he kept going out on the road as Trevor and Beth's number one troubleshooter. And it wasn't too far from Thea's folks, who lived in Sacramento. They could come up and visit or Thea and Ezra could easily scoot down the coast to see them.

The location was close to ideal, and they'd have the strength of an entire town full of bears and mer behind them. Ezra privately thought that might make Thea feel a bit more secure. She'd made incredible strides, but she would probably still be recovering from her ordeal for some time to come.

They took their time heading west to Washington State. The trip was something of a honeymoon for the newly mated couple. They stopped frequently and stayed in fancy hotels in each city they passed through, making love in big, soft beds and taking advantage of stately bathrooms with giant showers and one particularly memorable tub big enough for two.

Ezra spared no expense when it came to his new mate. He showered her with gifts—at least those small enough to fit in their saddlebags. He was making plans as he rode alongside her. Plans for the house he would build for her. A house big enough for the children they had discussed in the dark of the night after the most glorious lovemaking of his life. A little girl with Thea's eyes and gentle voice. Or a little boy who kept them hopping with his antics. Either, or both, would be welcome if the Goddess so blessed them.

There would also be a guest suite for Thea's parents to visit as often as they wished. And if they wanted to move to Grizzly Cove, too, Ezra would do everything in his power to talk the guys who ran the town into it. First, of course, he'd have to get permission to move in and buy land there himself, and—the biggest thing of all—he had to see if Thea liked it enough to want to live there.

He thought she would. The place could be a fresh start for both of them, surrounded by people he knew and trusted with his life. More importantly, he trusted them with Thea's life. Every one of the core group who had created Grizzly Cove were stand-up bears with their heads screwed on straight.

The Alpha bear, John Marshall, was a strategic genius and had led men in battle. Ezra would stand with Big John any day of the week. And Trevor was there with his new mate, Beth. Ezra had a feeling Thea would hit it off with Beth. Both women had been through so much to find happiness with their true mates. They had a lot in common, though, of course, Beth was a mermaid.

The closer they got to the coast, the more excited and nervous Ezra became. Would Thea like the town? Would she want to live there? If she did, would the bears accept them into the community? There were a lot of questions running through his mind, but he tried not to let it get him down. All things could be conquered, given enough time and the proper strategy. He just had to figure out how.

Thea sensed Ezra's edginess as they approached the small town hidden away on the Washington coast. The redwood forest they drove through was magnificent, but Ezra's mood was getting to her a little, and she couldn't truly relax and enjoy her surroundings. Was he worried about what his friends would think of her? Was he concerned she wouldn't fit in?

Thea was worried enough about that for both of them, but

she didn't want to give voice to her doubts. She didn't want Ezra to know that she was afraid of the reception she would receive from the other bears.

She'd grown up alone, in a family of loners. She hadn't ever really hung around with other bears. At least, not until recently. Ezra and the three brothers were the only other bear shifters she really knew besides her parents. She had no idea if the bears in Grizzly Cove would like her or shun her completely, and she was really nervous about finding out. Ezra's mood wasn't helping reassure her either.

When they drove through the little town at the apex of a wide cove, Thea was charmed by the quaint shops and multitude of little art galleries. The buildings were obviously new, but they had a sense about them that they were well-loved and happy places to live and work. There was a tingle of magic about the place that was somehow joyful.

Ezra didn't stop in the town but drove, instead, to the end of the strip of buildings that culminated with a hotel on the beach side of the street. He stopped in a parking spot big enough for both of their bikes to sit side by side. Thea got off her bike, stretching out the kinks in her muscles for sitting so long. They'd taken their time getting here, but it had been a long trip, regardless.

"This where we're staying?" Thea asked, trying to hide her nerves, which were growing even more taut now that they'd reached their destination.

"Yeah." Ezra nodded. "And it's also where Trevor and Beth are bunking down while their home is being built. You'll like them," he told her, as he had a few times before. "Trev's an old friend, and his mate, Beth, is a sweetheart." He unbuckled his saddlebags and grabbed Thea's, too, carrying them for her as he led the way into the hotel.

"Hey, Billy," Ezra called to the man behind the front desk. "My old room available?"

"Hey, Ez, long time, no see. And who's the lovely lady?" Billy's eyes sparked with interest.

"Billy Longknife, this is Thea Jackson. My mate."

A little thrill went through Thea when he said that. She noticed the way Billy's eyes widened, and then, his face broke into a giant grin.

"You don't say." Billy looked at them both speculatively. "Anybody else know about this?"

"Not yet," Ezra replied. "But I'm sure it'll get around town eventually." Ezra laughed as Billy nodded, and Thea got the idea that Ezra expected Billy to spread the gossip as soon as they were out of sight.

"Congratulations, man," Billy said, his tone sincere and somewhat emotional. "And to you, ma'am. Ol' Ez here is one of the good'uns."

Thea smiled at the other man, putting her hand on Ezra's arm. "That he is."

"Here." Billy tossed a key card to Ezra, and he snatched it out of the air in the blink of an eye. "Your old room is ready for you. Trevor and Beth are still next door. Their house is nearing completion, but it'll be a little bit yet before they move out."

"Thanks, Bill. We'll see you later," Ezra told the other man as he led the way down one of the hallways that spawned off the main entrance area.

They were heading toward the beach end of the building. Thea looked forward to seeing what kind of view their room might have. The cove looked incredibly picturesque. She couldn't help but steal glances at it as they'd ridden through town. She couldn't wait to walk along the shore and just...be.

Thea loved looking at the ocean, and she thought she was going to enjoy her time in this town on the edge of it. So far, she'd like what she'd seen of Grizzly Cove. Now, she just had to get over the hurdle of meeting the locals.

"Ezra!" A woman shouted from a short distance down the hallway, and Thea looked up to find a small woman coming toward them at a fast clip.

A much larger man was right behind her. The guys smelled of bear, but the woman wasn't quite like anything Thea had scented before. A little salty, perhaps. Was this a mermaid? She certainly was petite. At least compared to bear shifters. The woman was sized more like an average-sized human. Maybe a bit on the smaller size for a human woman, Thea revised her judgment as the woman walked right up to Ezra and gave him a hug.

And why was this other woman hugging her mate? Thea's bear half sat up and took notice. If that hug strayed from merely friendly into something more intimate, the bear was ready to swat Ezra back into line, but it didn't. It was pretty clear from both of their body language that the woman and Ezra were merely friends.

Thea met the strange man's gaze across the distance, Ezra and the woman between them. His gaze was calculating and seemed to miss nothing. Suddenly, Thea felt a bit more on edge. Would this bear shifter judge her as not fit to be in Grizzly Cove? Was he one of those who could make such a decision?

Ezra let go of the woman and turned to the man as the woman stood looking at Thea with her head tilted to one side, her smile cautious but still welcoming. Ezra held out a hand to the other man, and they hugged briefly, as bears often did, but it was a bit more of a bro hug with that back-slapping thing where they sort of bumped shoulders.

"I'm Beth," the woman said, showing no fear as she faced Thea. "You must be Theodora."

"Um…yeah. Hi. Call me Thea," she replied, caught off guard by the fact that the other woman seemed to already know about her.

Ezra and the other man ended their greeting, and both turned to look at the women. The man came to stand behind Beth and held out a hand to Thea.

"I'm Trevor. Ez has told us a bit about you, of course, but I'm glad to finally meet you," he said, his tone and expression friendly.

This was Ezra's friend, and the couple were his bosses. Thea recognized the names, but somehow, she'd pictured them older. Probably because of the business empire Ezra had told her about that they commanded.

"Nice to meet you, too," Thea said, returning the other bear shifter's handshake.

The couple seemed very nice on first impression. She hoped she didn't look too wrung out from the journey. She had hoped to be able to clean up a bit in the room before encountering too many locals—and especially these two, who were so close to Ezra.

"You guys just arrived, didn't you?" Beth said, seeming to look at the saddlebags Ezra had dropped in order to return her greeting hug. "We should let you settle in, but I hope you'll join us for dinner. Zak has his restaurant going full steam now, and he's added some really yummy seafood items to the menu for us. Do you want to meet there at about six?"

Ezra looked at Thea, and she could only nod. She wasn't quite sure what she was agreeing to, other than dinner, but seafood sure sounded good. It would likely be really fresh, considering they were on the coast.

"That would be great. We'll meet you there," Ezra said, answering for both of them.

The other couple headed off after a quick goodbye, and Ezra led Thea the few steps to the door of their room. He slid the key card over the lock mechanism, and the door clicked open.

The room was nice. Obviously new with fresh paint and sparkling finishes. And it was big enough for a bear shifter...or two.

"Trev and Beth have the room next door. I've been staying in this one whenever I'm in town," Ezra told her as he deposited their saddlebags on the table in the corner.

"They seem nice," she replied noncommittally. She wanted so much for his friends to like her, but she didn't want to let on how nervous she was about it all.

"They're great," Ezra replied, digging into his bags for a change of clothes. "We have just enough time for a quick shower." He turned back to her, smiling that sexy smile she'd come to know meant he was up for mischief. Delicious mischief of the sexy kind.

"Don't you mean a *quickie* shower?" she asked, feeling playful as she walked up to him and leaned in for a smooch.

"I like the way you think," he told her, putting his hands around her waist and drawing her close.

They undressed as they chivvied themselves toward the bathroom and its large, open shower by small moves. It was almost a dance as they took turns taking off various items of clothing from themselves and each other as they moved closer to their target. By the time they made it under the water, which Ezra set running before they got in, things were getting steamy—and that wasn't just the water.

Thea pushed Ezra back up against the side wall of the shower enclosure, loving the texture of his hot, wet skin under her hands and against her body. He was hard in all the right places, and he seemed to appreciate the areas where she was soft against him.

His hands stroked her breasts and played with her aching nipples as she explored his sculpted body. At one point, she sat down on the bench at the back of the shower and crooked her little finger for him to come close. He smiled with wicked delight as he stalked closer to her, and she bent forward to take him in her mouth.

She played with him, coaxing his reaction ever higher, using her blunt-tipped nails to scratch up and down the backs of his thighs. She knew from their past travels and encounters that he liked that. A lot.

A little bit of that treatment, and he growled, sweeping down to lift her into his arms and reposition them so that he was sitting on the wide bench and she was straddling him. Then, he joined them, and it was her turn to growl in appreciation.

The water pelted down on her back, just reaching her where they were positioned at the far end of the long shower stall. It blanketed her in warmth from behind while Ezra's solid presence kept her warm from the front. It was a delicious sensation all the way around. Ezra was turning her into a real fan of shower sex. It seemed to be one of his favorite places to make love, and she was quickly coming to understand why.

He thrust up into her as she moved to meet him. They strained against each other, and she knew this was definitely going to be a *quickie*, as she had teased him. First and foremost, she was hungry for him after hours of abstinence as they had driven the last leg of their journey here. It felt like she couldn't go more than a few hours without stopping to jump his bones these last few days. Maybe she was in heat…or maybe, her new mate had somehow addicted her to his lovemaking. She'd bet on the latter.

Second, they were expected for dinner, and she wanted to make a good impression, which meant she needed time to do her hair and maybe put some thought into her wardrobe— though she didn't have a whole lot with her because of saddlebag limitations. Still, she had a little black dress that ought to work nicely for a dinner out at a restaurant. It was a slinky thing that didn't take up a whole lot of room in her luggage, so it should still be in reasonable condition. She'd have to check and see if maybe hanging it up in the steamy shower would loosen any wrinkles.

But that was for later. Right now, her man was driving her wild, and wardrobe issues were the furthest thing from her mind. She rode Ezra like her Harley, giving no quarter and taking all he had to give. And that was a *lot*.

Ezra pushed her higher and higher, using his skilled fingers to play her body. Eventually, after he'd wrung a few hard, fast climaxes out of her, he moved his right hand to the apex of her thighs and began his master stroke. He knew just how to touch her now to set off not just fireworks, but nuclear explosions. She shouted her completion as her passions jolted toward the heavens. Then, he tensed along with her, and they rode to the stars together, on the flaming spear of light his explosive touch had caused.

The comedown was monumental, but she pushed his wet hair off his face and kissed him all over his stubbly cheeks before zeroing in on his lips.

"I love you, Ezra. I'm so glad you're my mate," she whispered, emotion riding high as her heart opened and love for him poured out.

Ezra's gaze softened, and the look he gave her filled all the empty places in her soul.

"I love you, too, Thea." He kissed her then—a kiss of promise and dreams for their shared future. A kiss of the deepest love a man could have for a woman. A kiss of souls and hearts and minds and animal spirits.

CHAPTER FOURTEEN

They were a tad late for dinner, but Trevor and Beth didn't mention it. They were welcoming and gracious, and Thea loved it when Ezra growled at the single bear shifter males who dared give her the once-over in her little black dress. He'd almost objected when she'd come out of the bathroom with her hair piled up in a—hopefully—stylishly messy bun, the LBD outlining her curves and the single pair of heels she'd allowed herself to pack for her road trip.

He'd growled low in his throat in approval, which made her feel even sexier. She realized he was having a little trouble with possessiveness and perhaps a spark of jealousy, but he'd have to learn to deal with it. She wasn't going to start walking around in sackcloth and ashes to please his possessive nature.

Then again, when some of the petite little mermaids started checking out her man as they walked through the busy restaurant, Thea got a little dose of what he must be feeling. Maybe they'd just stay in where nobody else could see them for a few years…until the jealous monster inside died down a little.

"You're gorgeous, Thea," Beth said, her bubbly greeting

going a long way toward soothing Thea's riled inner grizzly.

It was hard to be grouchy with Beth around. She seemed so intensely happy with her mate, and Trevor seemed like a steady, level-headed sort of bear. Thea liked them both very much, at least on first impressions. Then again, she'd probably been predisposed to like them after hearing about them both from Ezra. It was clear he was close friends with Trevor, and had been for a long time.

"I love your dress," Thea returned Beth's compliment. "And I wish I could learn how to do my hair like yours."

Beth laughed. "When you live underwater and have long hair, you learn a lot about braiding. I'd be happy to show you sometime."

"Thanks, I'd like that."

Their pleasant exchange set the tone for the rest of the dinner. It wasn't until after the sumptuous feast flavored with tangy Cajun spices that they got down to business.

"Thea, Ezra has told us a bit about your contribution to this last mission of his, and we want you to know how grateful we are to you for your input," Trevor began, speaking for the couple. "If you two want to make a go of this partnership, Beth and I can make it official and add you to the employee roster."

"You're offering me a job?" Thea blurted out her thoughts, perhaps unwisely. Had she sounded ungrateful? She hadn't meant it that way. "I mean… That's very kind of you. I suppose my answer is going to depend on what Ezra wants to do."

Beth looked at them both quizzically. Ezra cleared his throat as if he was suddenly uncomfortable.

"The thing is…" Ezra began in a subdued voice. "I hadn't planned to do this here, but you need to know…" He cleared his throat again, surprisingly nervous-sounding before he finally spit out what he'd been trying to say. "Thea and I are mates."

She loved it when he said that. The smiles that lit Trevor and Beth's faces were joyful, and congratulations were given and received. Trevor called for champagne, and it wasn't long before everyone in the room realized what they were celebrating. Ezra was a popular guy, and many of the men stood from their own tables and came over to slap him on the back and offer their congratulations to them both.

The simple dinner turned into an impromptu celebration as folks from every table in the place came over to offer their good wishes. Champagne flowed at Beth's request, and everyone joined in a toast to the new couple. Ezra looked abashed but really proud, which made Thea love him all that much more, if such a thing were possible. She already loved him so much she wasn't sure where her heart left off and his began. They were that in tune with each other.

Thea put away the fears that had been rattling around in her mind about the town and its people. If their honest happiness for the new couple in their midst was anything to go by, this town was one-of-a-kind in the best possible way. The people here didn't even know her yet, but they were welcoming her and celebrating the most joyous occasion in her life. If that didn't prove to her that she could be accepted in this town, nothing else could.

The only questions that remained were if Ezra truly wanted to settle down here and if the town council would be willing to grant them residency. She understood why the bears who ran the place wanted to keep it private, but she really hoped they'd allow two more to join them. Ezra was already friends with some of them, but they didn't know her. Would they let her move here? She certainly hoped so. But she and Ezra still hadn't really had a chance to talk over the specifics of their plans for the future.

"I hear congratulations are in order," a strong male voice boomed from behind Thea, from the direction of the front door to the restaurant.

She turned her head to find an imposing bear shifter male with a human-looking woman at his side, though there seemed to be something...magical...about her. A witch? Here? Thea's hackles rose as concern filled her. What was this? Hadn't she had enough trouble with mages for one lifetime?

She looked to Ezra, but he was grinning. He stood to meet the other man and held out his hand for a firm grasp and a quick bro hug as they drew together. Then, he escorted the man and his witch companion to their table to meet Thea. She rose, wanting to be ready for anything, though she really didn't understand what was going on here.

"Thea, my love, this is the Alpha bear of this town, John Marshall, and his mate, Urse. Folks, this is Thea Jackson, my mate." Pride and love filled Ezra's voice, and Thea tried not to worry. He was exuding confidence and friendship all over the place. He liked the couple—that was plain enough to see.

Maybe this witch was one of the good ones? Though, of course, Thea had never met one of those before. Still, if she could have dinner with a mermaid, then maybe white witches could exist, too.

Thea held out her hand to the other woman. When their fingers met, a tingle of magic passed along Thea's hand, and the woman smiled.

"Sorry. Sometimes, my magic does that when I meet a new shifter. It was just checking you out," Urse said with a friendly expression.

"Did I pass the test?" Thea half-joked back, not really sure what had just happened and feeling a bit unsteady in the strange situation.

She knew these two were the ruling couple of the town, but if Thea was going to be subjected to a mage of ill intent, she would think twice about wanting to live here.

"If you hadn't, they'd be carrying you out of here right about now." So. The human sorceress had claws, too.

"I'm not sure what you might have heard about me, but I've had a lot of trouble with mages in recent months. I'd really like to know what's going on here." Thea turned her concerned gaze to Ezra.

"It's cool, honey," he was quick to reassure her. "Urse is on our side. Beyond the shadow of a doubt." Ezra put his arm around Thea's shoulders, probably trying to calm her down. It worked. Her bear started to settle a bit from its ready stance, though it still watched the witch carefully.

"Miss Jackson." The other male was speaking to her now, and his presence was soothing, despite the strange situation. "Forgive me. I've heard a bit about what you went through, and I want you to know you're welcome in this town. We are open to any bear shifter who stands on the side of Light. And some Others, too. Like our mer friends and a few select magic users." He wrapped one arm around his mate's waist and pulled her into his side. It was clear from their body language that the two were deeply in love. "My mate is cautious," he went on. "She tries to protect me, and I'm afraid she was assessing you as a potential threat."

Thea shook her head. "I guess I'm flattered, then," she said honestly.

"Tonight is for celebration," John went on, doing a good job of smoothing over the little incident. "Congratulations on your mating, and please, don't let us interrupt your evening, though I hope you'll all come by the office tomorrow to give us a debrief on the situation in South Dakota. I'll be interested to hear more details."

"Sure thing, John," Ezra said, as Trevor nodded. It appeared they all knew more about each other and the mission Ezra and Thea had just come from than she realized.

The Alpha couple went off to their own table, and Thea and Ezra sat back down with Trevor and Beth. A moment later, the lights in the restaurant dimmed, and the chef walked out with a giant cake in his hands, covered in lit candles. The cake had writing on it, and when it got closer, she could see it had their names and a big, "Congratulations!"

Thea and Ezra blew out the candles, and then, the cake was cut up into pieces and handed all around the restaurant so everybody could join in the celebration. Thea was back to being overwhelmed by the generous spirit of the town and its people. The shifters—bear and mer alike—were fantastic. It remained to be seen if Thea could get along with the magical contingent, but if Urse was the only one, then maybe Thea could just avoid her.

The cake was delicious, but eventually, the party came to an end, and they took their leave of Beth and Trevor. Ezra escorted Thea back to the hotel at the other end of town. They'd walked to dinner, and the stroll back was lovely with the slight wind coming off the cove and the moonlight glinting on the water. It was truly beautiful.

"What do you think of the place so far?" Ezra asked as they strolled along in the faint light of the moon.

"It's very pretty. And the people seem really nice. I was a little surprised by the witch, though," she admitted, wondering what he'd say.

"I'm sorry, honey. I honestly didn't think anything about how you might react to her—or her to you. John must not have told her anything about you. I seriously doubt she'd have come on so strong if he had. Urse has a kind heart and a major protective streak where this town and her mate are concerned. I know she didn't mean any harm, and I bet she's going to feel really bad about challenging you that way once she knows more about your background. In her defense, she's still trying to figure out her role as Alpha female. She doesn't always understand shifter ways, but she tries hard, so the guys tend to cut her some slack. That, and everyone here owes her big for what she did for the town," Ezra put in. To Thea, that sounded like there was a story attached.

"What did she do?" she asked, enjoying the feel of Ezra's arm around her as they walked along.

He was very warm and comforting, even if she was struggling to understand his liking for a witch. Every contact Thea had ever had with a magic user had been bad. It would take her some time to see them in any other light.

"She and her sister are what is known as *stregas*. They're hereditary witches descended from an Italian line of wise women. Their grandmother is one, as well. The thing with Urse and her sister, Mellie, is that they're both immensely powerful, in their own ways. Urse does spells, and Mellie does potions. Both have put themselves on the line to protect the town."

"You've hinted at that before. What's going on here that the town needs so much protection?" Thea asked.

"They've got a little sea monster problem," Ezra astounded her by saying. At first, she thought he was joking, but he kept going. "There's a creature known as the leviathan. It's not of this realm, and it's pure evil. Damn thing was right up in the cove before Urse set wards against it. She had to do a series of powerful spells several days in a row, putting herself in range of the monster. She risked life and limb to create a safe zone in the cove for the mer and wards all around on land through which no evil can pass."

"You're serious." Thea shook her head.

"It happened before I came to town, but I've heard the story a time or two. It seems Urse is one of the very rare, very powerful mages that can cast permanent wards. Those protections she put around the town on land and in the water will last long after we're all gone. They're permanent. Master works, according to some." Ezra sounded admiring, and Thea tried to take in the implications of what he was saying. It seemed incredible.

"Then, her sister did a potion that pushed the creature far from the shore, not only of Grizzly Cove, but all up and down the coast and around the ring of fire," he went on. "She isolated the creature and its minions to the deep ocean, protecting the innocent on shore for many, many hundreds of miles of shoreline." Ezra shook his head. "It was pretty spectacular, from all accounts. Trust me when I say, those two *strega* sisters have done more to protect the people who live here than most of the bear shifters who came up with this cockamamie idea to form a town and disguise it as an artists' colony."

"So, that's why there are so many art galleries," Thea blurted out. At least one thing was making sense.

"Yeah. Everybody here is supposed to contribute some kind of art to the tourist trade that they expect to show up once the town is more established. The theory is to hide in plain sight. So far, it seems to be working like a charm, even if concentrating so many bears in one place brought about a bit of unexpected notice from things like the leviathan." Ezra stroked her shoulder with one hand as he snuggled her to his side. "But they're handling it. Every time something bad comes calling, the guys here face it together. It's good to have backup, and these guys are a fine team to have at your back when trouble comes calling."

"They seem very close knit," Thea replied, thinking aloud.

"Yeah, they are. Thing is, we could live here. If you wanted." He stopped walking and turned to face her, looking deep into her eyes. "I would build us a house, and you can design it any way you want. We could put down roots here, and if we're blessed with cubs, they could grow up with friends of their own kind."

"That really sounds wonderful," she agreed. "But give me a little more time. I want to see more of the town, and I want to check out that so-called Alpha female for myself a little closer. I trust your judgment, but I need to know if I'm going to have trouble every time she and I cross paths. That's something only I can evaluate."

"Fair enough." Ezra turned and started walking again, tucking her close to his side. He seemed disappointed, but she couldn't commit until she knew more about Urse and her magic.

CHAPTER FIFTEEN

The next morning, Ezra took Thea out to breakfast at a quaint little bakery that was seeing a brisk business. She recognized some of the people from the night before, and many stopped to wish them well.

Thea realized the cake they'd eaten last night must have come from here when she noticed another just like it in the display case. She complimented the woman behind the counter and found out that the bakery was run by three human sisters who had all found mates among the bear shifters of Grizzly Cove, one of whom was the owner and chef from the restaurant. When a celebration was called for, someone popped down the road to the bakery and picked up a cake.

Thea was very pleasantly surprised that the folks of this town had gone so far out of their way for her and Ezra. They'd turned what had been a regular dinner into a party when they'd heard about the new mating, and Thea had been incredibly touched by the gesture. Everyone had made her first evening in Grizzly Cove memorable in the best possible way.

Except maybe for the tiny run-in with the Alpha's witch mate. That was something that still needed to be resolved, but Ezra's explanation about the *strega* sisters and what they had done for the town had impressed Thea. Now, if she and this Alpha female could just come to some kind of understanding... Then, everything in this new town would be darn near close to perfect.

After breakfast, they walked over to the town hall, where, apparently, Ezra had set up the meeting the Alpha had requested the night before. He must've called while Thea had been getting dressed because they were ushered into a conference room where Trevor, Beth, John and a few others were already waiting for them. It looked like the meeting had been going on for a while before they got there, and Thea immediately noticed the Alpha's mate, sitting at his side, looking a little contrite.

Had they been discussing Thea and her somewhat disturbing past? She got the sinking feeling that maybe they had.

Still, nothing was said of it while the rest of the group said hello, and Thea and Ezra took the seats reserved for them at the big conference table. Ezra picked up the carafe of coffee on the table and poured two paper cups full, one for each of them, before things settled down.

What followed was a detailed debrief on what had happened in South Dakota from the time Ezra had run into Thea on the road, until they'd left to come here. Ezra handled most of the report but seemed glad to have Thea talk about some of their shared experiences.

He also coached her through her description of the final confrontation with Sarella from her point of view. The rest sat and listened, mostly, though they asked for more detail on certain points.

They were particularly interested in Thea's knowledge of Sarella. She gave them the details as best she could without revealing too much about her feelings on the matter—or so she hoped.

The people around the table were very professional and had been asking astute questions with no hint of emotion. Thea tried to be the same, even though it was pretty clear all the men, at least, had military backgrounds.

They'd probably heard and seen worse in their careers than Thea had been through, which made it somewhat easier to reveal how she knew what she did about Sarella. The other woman present, though... John's mate, Urse... She wasn't a combat veteran. She wasn't even a shifter. Thea found it impossible to look at Urse while she went into detail about Sarella and how Thea had first met her while being held prisoner by Bolivar.

Luckily, after the questions about Sarella were through, Ezra took up the narrative again. He told them about the local Alpha and making the job offer.

He then detailed the Alpha werewolf's remorse over being duped by Sarella and talked about some of the things Chase had told him about the woman and the garage that Thea hadn't known. He also mentioned the three bear shifter brothers, who seemed to be known to a few of the men in the room.

They took a quick break in the meeting after Ezra and Thea finished up their report. A few guys headed out to pick up snack trays that someone said had been delivered to the front desk. A few more walked around and stretched or made pit stops. Thea got up and walked toward the row of windows that looked out onto the cove. It really was pretty here.

"I hope you can forgive me." Urse's voice came from Thea's side.

How had the witch snuck up on her? And where was Ezra?

Thea spotted him off to one side, talking with two other men. Well, then. She was on her own, but she could handle this. Right?

"For what?" Thea decided to try to play this cool.

"For zapping you last night. I didn't intend to, you know.

It was just a little magical probe I sometimes use to try to get a quick read on new people. It's harmless. You just have some natural barriers that are a bit stronger than the average bear's. And I never would have attempted any magic around you had I known..." Urse trailed off, looking away as if mortified. "I'm really sorry."

"I haven't had the greatest experiences with mages," Thea said, feeling her way through this conversation. She thought Urse sounded very genuine and very contrite. Thea would accept the apology, but not pity. Thea's bear half snorted at the idea of being pitied by anyone. She was strong now. Not a bear needing anyone's pity.

Urse's gaze slid toward her mate and then back again to Thea. "John mentioned some of the problems you've had. I want you to know, just as there are good and bad people, there are good and bad magic users. My sister and I... Our entire line, really, has been sworn to the Light for generations." Thea remained quiet, wondering if she could really trust this woman. This mage. "We've made our home here. Found our mates here. And we'll do anything and everything in our power to protect those we love and keep this town free of evil." Urse seemed to straighten her spine. "I check out new people, and I'm not sorry for it, but I am sorry if it caused you discomfort. If you stay, in time perhaps, you'll come to find that not all mages are bad."

Hmph. The Alpha female was asserting her authority a little. Well, good for her. Thea's inner bear respected the woman more for the uncompromising stance.

"You have every right to defend and protect your home and your mate," Thea responded with absolute conviction. "I accept your apology and want you to know that I've been trying to put my past experiences behind me. I hope I've learned enough to keep an open mind, but like I said, my recent experiences with mages have been all bad."

"Maybe we can change that for you," Urse said with a smile. It looked like they were past the first hurdle and perhaps on their way to better understanding. Thea was glad.

John came over at that point and put his arm casually around his mate's waist. "Thea, I understand your parents live on the West Coast," he said in a friendly tone.

"Sacramento," she replied, wondering what might come next.

"You should invite them up here to see the town. Bears are always welcome, and Ezra tells me they haven't had a chance to really get to know him yet." John frowned a bit. "In the spirit of family harmony, you should probably fix that as soon as possible."

"My parents aren't..." How could she explain this without sounding disloyal? "I mean, you're all very dominant bears, and my folks...aren't. Part of the reason I left home was because, after what happened, I didn't really fit in with them anymore."

John nodded sagely. "You had a trial by fire. You'll find many of my men have had similar experiences. It changes you, and your bear. What didn't kill you made you stronger," he said quietly. "But they're still your parents. They love you, and it's important for their inner peace to see that you're happy and well mated. Invite them up. I promise, none of my bears will push them around. That's not how we are here. We're a family, not like some wolf Pack where they're constantly testing the pecking order. We're bears." He shrugged, as if that said it all.

And perhaps, it did.

Thea called her parents and invited them up to visit right after the meeting. By the afternoon of the following day, her mom and dad were driving through town on their way to the hotel. Ezra had reserved a room for them—at the other end of the sprawling building from his and Thea's room, at her request—and insisted on paying for it.

She realized Ezra was a little nervous about seeing her parents again and was trying hard to make a good impression. The last time he'd seen them was when they'd come to collect her from Lake Tahoe after he'd rescued her from Bolivar's basement torture chamber. She'd been very weak, but she remembered the way he'd held her and stayed with her, almost seeming like he hadn't wanted to give her up, even to her family.

He had, in the end, but she knew his concern for her welfare had made a big impression on her mother. Her father was quieter about it, but she sensed from his occasional comments that her dad had been very impressed by Ezra's strength and character. She'd told them about their mating by phone, of course, and both her father and mother had spent some time speaking with Ezra, but seeing them in person was different.

She hoped they would all get along and that their inner bears didn't make things difficult. Ezra was such a strong Alpha presence—as were most of the other bears Thea had met since arriving in town—that she was a little afraid of her parents' reactions.

Bears weren't like some other shifters. They usually preferred to gather only in small family units. The young struck out on their own early and usually only went back for the occasional visit.

Thea's situation was a little different since her abduction and rescue. She'd left her parents' home as a rather meek woman, for a bear shifter. She'd been more docile than most bears, and that was probably why she'd fallen prey to the human trafficking ring. She'd been naïve and easily duped, and she'd paid for that in Bolivar's basement of horrors over and over.

The end result of her survival was that she was a very different woman now. And a very different bear. She wasn't sure her old self would have been able to handle a mate like Ezra, but this newer, stronger version was a perfect match— as he was for her.

Perhaps, had they met before her ordeal, they would have been merely two ships passing in the night, neither one really noticing the other. She would never be sure, but it didn't really matter. She was who she was now, shaped by her experiences, as Ezra had been shaped by a lifetime of his own choices and circumstances. They were perfect for each other now, and that's what really counted.

She hoped her parents would see that and accept him—and her—the way they were now. She could never go back to being that meek little bear she'd been when she'd left home. Her parents knew that—had known that—from the moment she'd started to recover, in the safety of her childhood home.

While she couldn't wait to see them and give them big hugs and kisses, she was also apprehensive. She had grown in ways she wasn't sure her parents would ever be ready to understand.

As it turned out, all her worries were for naught. When her folks pulled up in front of the hotel, Thea and Ezra were there to guide them in. While her father parked the car, Thea's mother hopped out of the passenger seat, and she and her mom rushed toward each other, meeting in a big hug laced with happy tears.

She was peripherally aware of Ezra greeting her dad sometime later, but her mother's arms felt too good around her to leave easily. She shouldn't have worried. No matter what changes she or her bear had been through, her mother was still her mom. That would never change.

And when her dad came closer and wrapped his arms around her from behind, enveloping her in parental love, Thea's strong, independent Alpha bear basked in her parents' love. Thea might be Alpha now where everyone and everything else was concerned, but she would always be her parents' little girl.

Happy tears filled her eyes as she looked up to see Ezra watching them with a suspicious brightness in his own eyes. The big softy. He might be her mighty Alpha mate, but he clearly understood what was going on before his eyes. Thea mouthed the words that filled her heart, sending them to

Ezra and her family at the same time...
"I love you."

EPILOGUE

Thea's parents stayed in Grizzly Cove for a few weeks. During their stay, they threw the party to end all parties to celebrate their daughter's mating to a bear they were proud to induct into the family. Ezra's folks were long gone, but the guys he'd served with who now lived in Grizzly Cove stood up for him as his family during the brief mating ceremony presided over by the town's shaman, Gus, in a sacred circle of stones out on one of the points of the cove.

The mer put on a display of synchronized leaps from the water under a strict veil of secrecy, and the Cajun gourmet put together a feast fit for a king...or at the very least, a bunch of strong bear shifters. At the dinner that followed the ceremony, an official invitation was issued to not only Ezra and Thea, but to her parents, as well, to settle in Grizzly Cove, if they wished.

By that time, Thea had spent many hours mulling over the pros and cons of moving to the small town by the sea. She'd also had time to encounter both Urse and her sister, Mellie, several times and get to know them a little better. She'd been surprised to find that, while Urse was still a little scary, Mellie was a total goof in the best possible way. They'd hit it off, and Thea realized with some astonishment that she was well on her way to being BFF to a very powerful witch.

Would wonders never cease?

When Ezra broached the topic of building a home in the area while they were in bed later that night, after a glorious session of lovemaking, she already knew what her answer would be. Her mom and dad had already hinted to her that they were going to look around at nearby real estate with an eye toward setting up a summer cottage by the shore, if such a thing was possible. So, when Ezra asked if she would be comfortable setting up their permanent base in the town, she felt her heart lift.

"I feel more at home here than I thought I would," she told him honestly. "And I can see that you're in your element with men you respect and whom respect you in turn." She drew little circles on his shoulder, loving the way he made her feel, just by being him. "If they're serious about letting us move here—and I think they are—then, I think we'd be fools not to do so. This place is...really, really special."

Ezra kissed her, joy and a feeling of coming home filling her. Then, he lay back, snuggling her close and proceeded to discuss the kind of house they would build. Together.

Long after home design had been exhausted as a subject and they'd fallen asleep, nestled together, they woke again to make love and renew the passion that would last them a lifetime. A lifetime that would be filled with joy...and maybe some danger...and definitely an infinite amount of love.

*

Later that day, on the road heading out of Sturgis, three bear shifter brothers rode their bikes into the sunset. When they got to the crossroads, each turned in a different direction. It was time.

They'd helped Ezra and seen the magic that only a true mate could bring. They'd all been waiting to find the loves of their lives. Perhaps it was about time they set out in search of their mates. They'd talked about it in the days since Ezra and his mate had taken off for Grizzly Cove, and they'd come up with this plan.

One was going north. One was going east. And the other was going south. They would meet up again after they'd done their best to fulfill their quests, in that little bear shifter town by the sea on the West Coast. They knew now that they had an open invitation to visit Grizzly Cove, but they'd decided not to go until they'd at least tried to find mates on their own.

They said farewell and hit the gas on their beloved bikes. The brothers were about to find out what Fate had in store for them...

# # #

ABOUT THE AUTHOR

Bianca D'Arc has run a laboratory, climbed the corporate ladder in the shark-infested streets of lower Manhattan, studied and taught martial arts, and earned the right to put a whole bunch of letters after her name, but she's always enjoyed writing more than any of her other pursuits. She grew up and still lives on Long Island, where she keeps busy with an extensive garden, several aquariums full of very demanding fish, and writing her favorite genres of paranormal, fantasy and sci-fi romance.

Bianca loves to hear from readers and can be reached through Twitter (@BiancaDArc), Facebook (BiancaDArcAuthor) or through the various links on her website.

WELCOME TO THE D'ARC SIDE…
WWW.BIANCADARC.COM

BOOKS BY BIANCA D'ARC

Brotherhood of Blood
One & Only
Rare Vintage
Phantom Desires
Sweeter Than Wine
Forever Valentine
Wolf Hills
Wolf Quest

Tales of the Were
Lords of the Were
Inferno

Tales of the Were – The Others
Rocky
Slade

Tales of the Were – Redstone Clan
The Purrfect Stranger
Grif
Red
Magnus
Bobcat
Matt

String of Fate
Cat's Cradle
King's Throne
Jacob's Ladder
Her Warriors

Gifts of the Ancients
Warrior's Heart

Guardians of the Dark
Half Past Dead
Once Bitten, Twice Dead
A Darker Shade of Dead
The Beast Within
Dead Alert

Grizzly Cove
All About the Bear
Mating Dance
Night Shift
Alpha Bear
Saving Grace
Bearliest Catch
The Bear's Healing Touch
The Luck of the Shifters
Badass Bear
Loaded for Bear
Bounty Hunter Bear

Tales of the Were ~
Grizzly Cove Crossroads
Bounty Hunter Bear

Tales of the Were ~ Were-Fey
Lone Wolf
Snow Magic
Midnight Kiss

Tales of the Were ~ Howls
Romance
The Jaguar Tycoon
The Jaguar Bodyguard

Dragon Knights
Maiden Flight
The Dragon Healer
Border Lair
Master at Arms
The Ice Dragon
Prince of Spies
Wings of Change
FireDrake
Dragon Storm
Keeper of the Flame
Hidden Dragons
Sea Dragon

StarLords
Hidden Talent
Talent For Trouble
Shy Talent

Irish Lullaby
Bells Will Be Ringing

Wild Irish
Wild Irish Rose *(Irish Lullaby)*

Sassy Ever After
A Touch of Sass

More than Mated
The Right Spot

Resonance Mates
Hara's Legacy
Davin's Quest
Jaci's Experiment
Grady's Awakening
Harry's Sacrifice

Jit'Suku Chronicles ~ Arcana
King of Swords
King of Cups
King of Clubs
King of Stars
End of the Line
Diva

Jit'Suku Chronicles ~ Sons of Amber
Angel in the Badlands
Master of Her Heart

WWW.BIANCADARC.COM

CPSIA information can be obtained
at www.ICGtesting.com
Printed in the USA
LVOW03s1500180418
573963LV00001B/236/P